Hoffer

Also by Tim Glencross

Barbarians

Hoffer

Tim Glencross

JOHN MURRAY

First published in Great Britain in 2017 by John Murray (Publishers)
An Hachette UK Company

1

A CIP catalogue record for this title is available from the British Library

ISBN 978-1-444-79759-6
Ebook ISBN 978-1-444-79761-9

Typeset in Sabon MT by Hewer Text UK Ltd, Edinburgh
Printed and bound by Clays Ltd, St Ives plc

John Murray policy is to use papers that are natural, renewable
and recyclable products and made from wood grown in sustainable
forests. The logging and manufacturing processes are expected to
conform to the environmental regulations of the country of origin.

John Murray (Publishers)
Carmelite House
50 Victoria Embankment
London EC4Y 0DZ

www.johnmurray.co.uk

Part I

I

Perhaps because Lady Antonia Highclere couldn't count on her husband – when she was entertaining, which was most evenings, Harold Highclere dined in another part of the house and was famously in bed by nine o'clock – she tended to put me next to her difficult guests.

On my right was the Japanese wife of the new Italian ambassador. She was young and spoke little English. (*L'ambasciatore* had a habit, according to Roland Turner, of remarrying at least once during each diplomatic posting.) At one stage things became so desperate I found myself reviving my Italian, an unsteady combination of Spanish and half-remembered phrases from opera. My remarks were each greeted with wide-eyed exclamation: they must have had an unintended melodramatic quality, but I began to suspect that her grasp of the language of Dante was not a million miles superior to my own.

The countess from Luxembourg seated to my left was a Singer Sargent beauty, with veiny translucent skin and a nose that finished in a discerning point. When she asked what I did for a living I pretended to mishear, and said, 'William Hoffer, pleasure to meet you,' even though we'd already been introduced. This wasn't because of any wish

to embarrass the countess so much as an old habit of evad-
ing the question of my occupation. Usually I made vague
reference to the family business in Ohio, and smiled and
changed the subject if the other person hadn't realised I
was American. If, as now, my interlocutor insisted on knowing what I did here in London, I'd reply I was a sort of
adviser to my friends.

'. . . But on *what*, exactly, do you advise?'

'Mostly philanthropic matters,' I said. My cheek muscles
had started to ache just a touch. 'The occasional art
acquisition . . .'

'If I could afford him,' Antonia smiled from the other
end of the table, which had suddenly gone quiet, 'I'd have
William advise me on everything.' Everyone knew Harold
was one of the last really rich locals. Or not quite local: his
father was a South African who'd made a fortune in
diamonds. Ingrid Vowles – known as Ingy or sometimes (by
her enemies) Harpy, and a rare constant of Antonia's
coveted inner circle – once told me Harold's real surname:
it was something Afrikaans-sounding.

The countess's interest surged visibly. 'And I think you
are not married?'

I didn't know if it was her continental phrasing or that I
radiated a sense of bachelordom.

'How is this possible?' she demanded to know.

Sensing the attention of the hostess, I frowned as if giving
the question perhaps unprecedented scrutiny. I imagined
explaining to the table at large the business aspect – that
remaining unattached meant others were productively
attracted or curious or pitying. I was tall with a Roman
nose and thick German-blond hair, and swam every day,

but as anyone could see I'd soon enough be leaving 'handsome' for 'distinguished'. Plenty of my rivals could advise on which art to acquire and charities to patronise, and more still were capable of mopping the brows of anxious Zurich bankers. Meanwhile I had a housekeeper, a (rented) Onslow Square address, an account at Berry Brothers, membership of the Imperial Club; but no money in the sense that someone like Nikolai or even most of those present would understand it. No money in the *ordinary* sense, was more or less the truth of the situation. Certainly no professional qualifications; no pension plan. What I possessed was 'charm' and the sort of connections which appealed to my clients' vanity and which cumulatively, over time, constituted a form of insurance. (Walking off with the motherland's natural resources didn't protect one from being poisoned – rather the opposite in fact – but being pictured in *Tatler* with the Duke of Kent just might.) Charm and connections were intangible enough assets without going around sleeping with people, who then hated you or, worse, claimed you.

'Antonia . . .' I said, after dinner.

'You're leaving, I know.'

'Very sensible,' said Roland, joining the trio of women I had myself just approached. 'I know for a fact Antonia was about to introduce you to a "socialite turned filmmaker".'

'Roland is the worst person you will ever meet.' Ingy clasped the upper arm of a blonde girl with bulbous eyes and a general air of malicious insecurity. If she was the former socialite in question she might have spurned a promising career. 'Wouldn't you say, William?'

In spite of careful make-up and endless rounds of laser-ing and peeling, Ingy's cheeks remained stubbornly pitted. I smiled, not widely – it wasn't my role to be wicked – and met her gaze. I considered them her redeeming feature but knew a single glance at her pockmarks had finished previous social careers.

I said, 'Today's *Financial Times* describes him as an "angel".'

'A *business* angel,' corrected Roland in an offended tone. 'Speaking of which . . .'

'I hope you're not going to talk shop,' said Ingy. 'It's bad enough the countess has spent the evening asking everyone what they do for a job. You know she was a travel agent in another life?'

'Are you coming to my Noma-at-Claridge's thing, after *Don Quixote*?' said Antonia, while a familiar reverential hush fell on those around her.

I said I was looking forward to it. Like the hostess herself, the little hesitancy in Antonia's voice was winning despite the cold calculation at its heart – people with no interest in either foraged foods or opera had all evening been angling for an invitation to join the party tomorrow. This was rumoured to include a Spanish royal as well as a Hollywood producer; the joke going round was that the latter was desperate to make a biopic of Harold.

'Is it true they're flying live ants over?' asked the blonde girl, still held in Ingy's clutch.

'Conversation-wise,' said Roland, 'I suppose there's not much to choose between the average first-class passenger and a Danish ant.'

'Perhaps you should downgrade!'

'If you wish to avoid causing offence,' Ingy advised the girl, with a faint sense this horse may have already bolted, 'the trick is to be like William and *always* leave early. Always show up, and always leave early.'

2

It was a balmy June evening so I decided to walk back to Onslow Square. Despite the heat, I was looking forward to a bath and the glass of Mouton Rothschild I'd pour myself once the coffin-sized lift (less endearing to my mostly absent Emirati and Uzbek neighbours) deposited me at my fifth floor apartment. *Flat*, rather. I tried to be disciplined with my language: it was 'shed-yool' never 'skej-ool'; 'anglicise' never 'anglicize'. In fact there was nothing vulgar or un-English about the '-ize' spelling, but I had no specific interest in such matters. *Vivre en bourgeois et penser en demi-dieu*, that was Flaubert's advice, whereas I'd lived like a demigod and now aspired to think like a bourgeois.

I hadn't yet shut the front door when Mrs Belsey – a sprightly octogenarian on the ground floor and the building's last remaining native – appeared in the hall. She also happened to be my landlady, though on the infrequent occasions her name came up in conversation I referred to her simply as my 'neighbour'. Of course no one imagined that at the age of fifty-one I might still be someone's tenant.

'Oh, *hello*, William.'

There was a hint of grandmotherly admonishment in her voice, as if I had missed my curfew. She explained that my goddaughter had rung her buzzer by mistake. I was obviously running a little late, so she'd lent the girl the keys to my flat.

Until his recentish death, the owner's keys were always kept by Mrs Belsey's husband. John Belsey had been a reticent former Navy man whom I thought might – if it came to it, which I hoped it wouldn't – withstand a degree of physical interrogation. The passing of the keys to the custody of Judy Belsey made me uneasy, as did the nagging fear that she might at some point overcome her English squeamishness and broach the subject of my rent, which had for years been dramatically below the market rate. Likewise, I was permanently afraid her grim daughter Annabel, with whom she seemed to have fortuitously distant relations, might finally succeed in convincing her to sell my lodgings.

'I thought it would be safer, you know, than have the girl wait in the square . . .'

'No, you're quite right. Thank you so much, Mrs Belsey.'

There had been an almost comic dissonance between the elderly woman's comforting tremulous voice, with its faint slur (from a stroke; she was teetotal), and the danger of her message. I wasn't expecting a visitor, and no one who knew me would call unannounced after nine. I had, more to the point, no goddaughter.

While careful I wasn't obsessive about security. If I ever had a serious lapse of judgement, or – as now, perhaps – some ghost of the past returned, a sophisticated alarm system or panic room wouldn't make a difference. For that reason I didn't consider turning and bolting from Onslow Square. What would happen then? I could have gone to Nikolai, but discovered my pride wouldn't allow it.

The absence of noise or movement inside the flat, coming after the little lift's hydraulic groan, was more eerie than usual: a slight shift in air density already announced a foreign presence. The hallway and sitting room were dark but there were lights on in the kitchen. Despite the gloom I noticed a slim volume jutting from one of the bookshelves. It was Octavio Paz's *The Labyrinth of Solitude*. For a second I wondered if Agustina, my housekeeper, had capriciously taken a look at the volume while cleaning that afternoon.

In the kitchen I found a girl of perhaps seventeen or eighteen years old. She was standing so diffidently that exit-via-the-window didn't seem ruled out. Her clothes were designer and WASPy: what you'd expect of a rich Latin teenager with no interest in fashion whose nearest high street was the King's Road. Though my greeting was natural enough I didn't feel the onus was on me to introduce myself, and felt a flicker of irritation when the silence swelled and my visitor wasn't prompted to speech.

Finally, I asked, 'Are you a tea person?', and busied myself with filling the kettle and then finding the pot and strainer. 'Perhaps you prefer it with lemon. I once asked a waiter for *té con leche* – this was in Colombia, a little place called Agua Clara. A long time ago. The waiter returned with a glass of warm milk with a Lipton teabag swirling around in it. We both laughed when we saw each other's faces.'

The girl was keeping her eyes firmly trained on the floor, but I had the impression she was listening intently.

I continued, 'But you're I think from Mexico.'

Using my Kramer knife – something of a treasured possession, with its snakewood handle and $500-an-inch patterned Damascus blade – I sliced a lemon which Agustina had left in the fridge. I diced it and set the table with cups and saucers and a jug of milk. 'I'm from North America myself – though I've been here so long people tend to assume I'm English, which I am, if one goes back far enough, at least on my mother's side.' After pouring the boiled water into the teapot I took a seat at the kitchen table.

In a slightly firmer tone I asked the girl her name.

'Diana Domínguez Saavedra.' Her voice cracked slightly on the initial 'a'.

'A Galician name,' I said. 'Of course before independence Jalisco was part of Nueva Galicia.'

With endearing pride Diana confirmed she was from the state of Jalisco.

'Yes, I know your father.'

'*Está desaparecido*,' she said in a breathless burst. 'He is missing.'

3

The first thing to be said about Diana Domínguez Saavedra, which I was careful to ignore or at least defer full acknowledgement of, was her looks. Even after a little time to gather my thoughts it seemed prudent to focus on her imperfections. For a start she was a fraction too short for the catwalk. There was also a touch of the Aztec about the way her arrowhead nose fanned at the tip: the effect was in a way magisterial, but perhaps not in Mexico, remembering Rafael Domínguez Saavedra's boorish tales of noble Spanish ancestors. Likewise her mestiza complexion, while no darker than an Italian's after August in Viareggio, probably wouldn't be admired in New World jockey clubs. Her black hair had been pinned up in a slightly Frida Kahlo-ish manner which if intentional was cruel, given Diana's far more orthodox beauty – one felt ashamed for not regretting the absent monobrow and wheelchair and bristly upper lip.

When she first told me her name I assumed she was here on summer vacation. Perhaps Rafael liked the idea of sending his daughter on a European grand tour, and there was a spinster aunt hiding away in a nearby Hilton. Or, more likely, an older cousin who'd got past the door at Boujis and left Diana to wander the neighbourhood. I was slightly puzzled and not delighted that Rafael would without warning recommend his daughter pay me a visit. It was true that if he'd wanted to get in touch he would have found my landline was unlisted. Nor did I own a mobile telephone or email address: an aperçu along the lines that possession of those things implied a failed life had been attributed to me, quite falsely, though I'd learned early on that no one maintained a full social diary by being easy to get hold of.

Possibly Rafael didn't know or couldn't remember my number in Onslow Square, so was unable write me a letter. (I had the impression Mrs Belsey's wasn't the only buzzer Diana had tried.) Or perhaps he simply couldn't be bothered. The last time he and I had been in contact the ink was barely dry on the Managua accords and Diana not even born. Back then, I'd done little more for Rafael than make a few representations on behalf of Domínguez Saavedra Constructora S.A. for a government contract for building new state prisons. I was aware that the surging demand for new detention facilities was at least in part down to the activities of the cartels through which I'd acquired the contacts in the Mexican administration. Ironies like these weighed heavier from Kensington, displaced from the larger context of the activities of my paymasters, who had blessed the alliance between Medellín and Guadalajara and then allowed both organisations to get wildly rich moving their product from Colombia to the north, via Mexico, in exchange for supporting the Contras. I happened to know the *narcotraficantes* had kept their end of the bargain, flying planes full of medicine, weapons and cash to Honduras and Nicaragua; just as I knew that those same cartel planes 'refuelled' at secret landing strips in Mexico before taking off again for Miami. The local DFS operated the landing strips but they effectively reported to the CIA. *Los gringos te hacen y los gringos te deshacen*: the gringos make you and they break you. Soon enough the problem wasn't ragtag Leninists running round Central America but the narco monsters the United States had helped create.

During my time in Mexico City I had an apartment with a rooftop balcony not far from the Zócalo. I went to dinner parties attended by Carlos Fuentes and expats who claimed to have been on drinking terms with Malcolm Lowry. When Béatrice Rochefort, the film actress, stayed at the French embassy she'd summon me for a gossip. (I'd barely speak.) Everyone assumed I was some sort of spy, and genially declined to make further enquiries.

By the end of the eighties the George H.W. Bush administration was making noises about extraditing cartel heads to the United States. Félix Gallardo was arrested in 1989. A few years later Escobar was killed and the centre of power moved north from Colombia, to Boschean effect, but at that point I was already in London.

When Diana made her unannounced visit I had no desire to revive my contacts in that part of the world. The Agency kept my name out of the senate commissions, but made it clear that they wouldn't (and couldn't) restrain the DEA if I ever got mixed up in that business again. More importantly, it would have displeased Nikolai.

Despite my remarks about my ancestry I didn't insist on the tea. Instead we took the bottle of Mouton Rothschild into the sitting room. Diana accepted less than half a glass; to settle both our nerves I took a firm sip while she watched, I suspected, for signs I might lose consciousness or start convulsing on the floor.

After blurting out the news about her father she'd become shy and incommunicative again. It was clear we'd have to return to the subject via a slightly circuitous route, so while the alcohol made its way into my bloodstream I mentioned the Octavio Paz book.

She coloured. 'I'm sorry. I shouldn't have touched it.'

'That's quite all right. He writes rather beautifully of Mexican identity comprising masks behind masks. The reticence – I think Paz calls it *hermetismo* – inherited from both the Spanish and Indian cultures.'

'I hated it.'

This wasn't the response I'd expected. 'Oh?'

'It's everything that's wrong with my country,' she said, very formally, like a guest on a BBC news show. Then she undercut herself by adding, 'Or almost everything. This idea Mexican women are no more than brainless idols.'

Diana had again gravitated towards the window, though in other respects she seemed to have relaxed a little. Behind her the trees in the railed square garden were almost black. I remembered my thwarted plan to be in the bathtub by now.

I'd revised my guess about the grand tour. 'You're at boarding school in London?'

'Since September – the Liceo Lope de Vega? It's here in Kensington.'

'Yes, I know it. The Lope de Vega has a good reputation.'

'I have exams next week: the *bachillerato*,' Diana added with touching gravity, as if I might have read about this in *Time*.

'Please tell me about the situation with your father . . . Start from wherever makes sense.' I gestured to the William IV sofa, a recent and unwisely expensive acquisition. 'It's not quite as uncomfortable as it looks.'

Diana perched tentatively. As I perhaps already knew, she began, her father was an engineer with his own construction company in Mexico City, with offices in Guadalajara and Matamoros. It was difficult to tell since they were living on different continents and spoke infrequently – she emphasised how busy she had been with exam revision – but lately his manner had been strange. He would end a call abruptly, or else talk at length on subjects he'd never discussed before: business debts; distressing details about the final stages of her mother's illness; the latter's terrible regret that the cancer treatment had left her infertile and Diana sibling-less. Then a week ago he'd called her out of the blue from a cell-phone number she didn't recognise. She'd thought this was unusual, not least as they usually communicated via Skype. It was a brief conversation, during which he sounded manic. He made her promise that if anything were to happen to him she must find William Hoffer of Onslow Square.

'He said you were brilliant – more than that, a good man. A *caballero*.' She smiled in shy acknowledgement of the Spanish word, with its hint of Golden Age drama. I considered joking that Rafael always had terrible judgement, before deciding it was too true to be in good taste. 'I thought he was drunk,' she continued, 'or on some new medication. He's had different treatments since my mom died.'

'And you haven't heard from him since that call?'

Diana shook her head. 'When I phoned his office the secretary told me he hadn't been seen for a week. She said this had happened before recently – he wouldn't turn up to work for a few days and during that time his phone would be switched off. But when she discovered I couldn't get hold of him either she became worried and said she was going to call the police. *Así que . . .*' Diana concluded, with a floundering shrug, 'probably it's nothing, and he'll call tomorrow. But I wanted to know if he'd been in contact with you – if you even existed, that is.'

When I told her I hadn't spoken to her father in years she flinched a little. 'The fact he particularly wanted you to find me suggests he's in trouble with some bad people. If so, it won't be safe for you to return to Mexico, even if the school and consular authorities say they want to send you back,' I added vaguely.

'I don't understand' – there was tightness in her voice and her knuckles blanched where they gripped the sofa's scroll finish – 'what sort of "bad people"?'

'I don't want to alarm you.' Then, '*Los de siempre.*'

Relief spread across her face. 'You think my father is a *drug dealer*?' she said, with an incredulous laugh. 'He's an engineer – he builds highways!'

'I know Rafael has certain connections, or did at one time.'

In Spanish she asked how I could be sure.

'I'm afraid I made the introduction.'

'Which cartel', she said, 'is my father supposed to be involved with?'

After a longish silence Diana stood up. Watching her replace the un-sipped wine glass on the coffee table, I noticed the care she took, despite everything, not to spill its contents or break the stem.

I said, 'Perhaps Rafael has heard something about my friends here in London. They can't help you, I'm sorry.'

'It's *you* who needs help! *Estás loco*. I recommend you to find a doctor.'

I hesitated for perhaps a few seconds before following Diana into the corridor. 'Please listen. If a man called Héctor Comala from the embassy – the Mexican embassy – comes looking for you, be perfectly normal and polite but don't agree to go anywhere with him.' She had slid inside the lift's folding shutter door and was pressing the ground-floor button with some urgency. 'Instead you should come straight back here – leave your mobile phone behind, so you can't be tracked; if I'm out at the time my housekeeper, Agustina, will let you in. Or use the spare keys Mrs Belsey gave you – I think you must still have them. Héctor Comala, remember the name.' In my final glimpse of Diana – with the shadow-filled worry line in her forehead, her hooded downcast eyes and unloosened wisps of hair – she reminded me of Caravaggio's Virgin, holding the infant Christ as she stepped on a serpent.

4

The day after my conversation with Diana I wasn't surprised Nikolai wanted to see me. For one thing I knew his people had installed recording devices in my flat. (I didn't flatter myself as unique in this respect; the Stasi might have admired Nikolai's surveillance operation.) It was regrettable to have to break my word to Antonia, and I was sorry in particular to miss the *Quixote* performance, but a driver arrived to collect me and that was that.

A storm sat over France and the propeller aircraft was thrown around a little. The sole cabin crew had wine on his breath and an unhealthily florid complexion beneath his carefully maintained suntan. He leant against the overhead locker in a parody of a debonair pose and filled me in – the pilot had wisely barricaded himself in the cockpit – on the various phases of his aviation career. He was gratified by my interruptions for more whisky, which he attributed to the turbulence.

It was early enough in the summer that the evening warmth felt thin and provisional; perhaps a jacket would be required before midnight. A Spaniard with a placard bearing my name was waiting to take me to Ciutadella, on the other side of the island. It was about an hour's drive. He glowered when I referred to it as 'Ciudadella' and on the way I noticed many of the street signs and place names had been changed from Castilian to Catalan, though many of the 'Spanish' names were themselves of Moorish derivation, after the arrival in the tenth century of the Córdoban caliphate. Thus what I knew as Binibeca, with its Arabic 'son of' prefix, was now Binibèquer.

The man dropped me at the main plaza, giving me the name of the restaurant on the harbour where I was to meet Nikolai in an hour. I must have been feeling sentimental in some unfocused and rather foolish way, because I wandered towards the cathedral in search of a cafe whose sole virtue was that I'd been there some years earlier.

I found the place with almost disappointing ease. It was brightly lit with a long mirror along the wall, and loud football commentary from the TV above the bar. The handful of local patrons – they must have been about my age, but looked about a hundred – gave little impression of being interested in the match.

I took a table outside in the sloping pedestrianised street. The cinema opposite was still in use, which was somehow pleasing. A waiter arrived and I ordered coffee. He ignored the group of university students crowded round the table next to me, but they seemed happy enough smoking and chatting excitedly about upcoming exams (or so I gathered; they spoke mostly in Menorquín). Two Guardia Civil, hardly more than boys, strolled past sharing a joke, while a pharmacist stood outside his shop watching the evening throng with arms crossed as though grimly sizing up maladies.

'So sorry – they were meant to be in bed *hours* ago!'

Even before I realised that the petite woman at the table in front was addressing me, I had registered her familiar Midwestern intonation. Not far from my elbow a pair of blond boys, perhaps four and six years old, were clashing toy robots. I glanced at their bowl haircuts and round indistinguishable faces.

'They think they're little Europeans. Won't go to bed till past midnight.'

This must have been the woman's husband. He was tall with sandy hair and a bulky frame that he probably carried off in a work suit. The polo shirt he wore now was black; the slimming shade suggested a certain sensitivity beneath his bluff demeanour. Or perhaps his wife picked out his leisurewear.

'That's quite all right,' I said.

'Pay up now, honey.' The man's grin was broad and faintly challenging, and directed at me.

The wife sounded embarrassed. 'We – I – thought you might be American. I have a cousin in Minnesota who looks just like you.'

'Apologies, *old man*,' the husband said. He gestured to his wife. 'We're at that point of the vacation – nothing left to talk about except the people around us.'

'When did you arrive?'

'Day before yesterday.' His laugh drew glances from the students, but there was an alertness about him that made me wonder if he was playing the rube.

'I see.' I smiled, and turned back to my coffee.

'Where in England are you from?'

'Pardon?'

'Your accent is British. I was wondering where you're from.'

'I live in London.'

'Uh-huh. We were there just last year. What part?'

I took out a five euro note from my wallet. 'I'm sorry, I was just leaving. Enjoy your holiday.'

'Bye then,' said the man, with a toothy grin. The wife was calling after her boys and I saw – not self-pityingly, simply as one does – that she'd already forgotten me.

The restaurant was one of the blander ones along the quayside and empty of regular patrons. Nikolai was in the far corner – though like Mao, as Kissinger observed, his position became the centre of any room. A table near the entrance and another not far from the Russian were occupied by his minders.

He continued eating while a waitress set my place. Without consulting me she served a portion of the paella dish already on the table and poured some white wine from a full carafe, before filling the other glass with sparkling water. A sip of the wine confirmed it was undrinkable.

'William.' His voice was always gentler than one expected.

We talked a little about the Auerbachs he had recently donated to the Tate. Choosing my moment carefully, I reminded him of the reception in his honour at the beginning of next week. Nikolai frowned at the table with childish petulance. His silver hair had been recently cut short and swept back, I noticed, with no attempt to cover where it was receding: it brought out the heaviness of his features, and the ugly brown tan.

24

'The parties', he said, dismissively, 'are your thing.'

'I don't know. Some would say I'm a recluse.'

'A sociable recluse.' He jabbed at my plate with his knife hand. 'What about the paella?'

'Oh, it's fine,' I said blandly. The rice lacked any hint of saffron, but I knew he had little interest in food. Instead I asked after a prospective joint mining venture in one of the less-regulated parts of Asia. A feted City dealmaker and some of the partners in Nikolai's own investment company had been convinced it was a terrific prospect, and were keen to move quickly. Without knowing much about it I'd suggested caution. Nikolai ended up insisting on a pause while an army of lawyers and tax accountants performed further rounds of due diligence.

'We found problems. A billion-dollar purchase of a single iron-ore mine.'

'That seems a lot.'

'It was non-producing.' He sipped sparkling water; his paella was by now abandoned.

I didn't want to give the impression I was searching for praise. 'Geoffrey Ireland, the earl, was saying Mallott Hall used to have a cricket pitch in its grounds. I wondered if it might be worth getting it going again, as a sort of gesture to the locals. We could host an annual charity match or perhaps invite a nearby club to use it for the odd fixture.'

'You know something about cricket?'

'I follow it a little.'

'This means you are an expert; though perhaps not with the American sports.' There was a sardonic glint beneath his heavy eyelids.

25

'It actually wasn't too long ago', I said, 'that baseball supplanted cricket in the United States.'

Nikolai thought for a moment. 'After the First World War.'

'In fact, it was in the wake of the Civil War – baseball became the patriotic choice.'

He talked for a bit about Mallott Hall: problems with his gardeners, the security arrangements. I didn't push the cricket idea. He seemed displeased about something. I worried that my Civil War comment had counted against me, by reminding Nikolai he couldn't altogether trust a man who wasn't loyal to his native sense of time. (The 1860s were not really recent in the American way of thinking.) This mistake might then bleed into the conversation to follow, so that from a throwaway remark I'd managed to magnify Nikolai's concerns and weaken my position.

'I've had a visitor.' I gathered I was to continue, so went on, 'There's not much to add to what you'll already know. I haven't spoken to the girl's father in years. They helped him win some construction contracts. In return they might have been putting money through his business. This was all a long time ago.'

' "They" . . . ?'

'The Ortega brothers. Well, just Igor now.'

Nikolai heard this news impassively, though he left an extra beat before saying, 'You think now he has stolen from Igor Ortega.'

'It would be my guess.' Turning informant would have been the smarter, less avaricious betrayal, and therefore less in keeping with the man I remembered. Besides, if he'd made a deal with the Mexican or US authorities there might have been a plan to protect his daughter, instead of Rafael's rather desperate advice that she find me.

'The wife died.'

I nodded. 'I'm afraid Rafael wasn't especially clear-headed to begin with.'

Nikolai understood the situation clearly – that these days the Ortega cartel used many additional channels to launder money, that it was a surprise Rafael had lasted so long, and that despite his relative insignificance he would be dealt with *pour encourager les autres*.

One of the minders had lit a rolled-up cigarette made with black tobacco. The smoke had a damp, almost tea-like flavour. I could hear the waitress in accented English explaining to a German couple that the restaurant was closed for a private function.

'What are you going to do?'

'The girl preferred not to believe my theory about her father. I don't think she'll come back.' I was conscious, more than usual, of Nikolai's appraisal.

'How did she enter your apartment?'

'She told my elderly landlady' – there was no point speaking vaguely of my 'neighbour' with Nikolai, who kept such a close watch over my affairs – 'that she was my goddaughter. It wasn't quite the truth. I'd left Mexico before she was born.'

His silence was telling. If she was willing to lie to Mrs Belsey, there were questions over her claimed predicament, and as a result there was no cause to be sentimental about it, let alone become personally involved. As it was he thought I'd told Diana too much at my flat, and would have been positively displeased if had he known what I'd gone on to say in the corridor. Of relevance to the Russian was the hundred billion or so barrels' worth of untapped shale oil and gas in Mexico, together with the recent legislative reforms opening up the state oil monopoly. The cartels – their extreme violence and propensity to siphon off millions of barrels of oil from existing state pipelines – were an impediment to what would otherwise be a gold rush for international investors. Put simply, Nikolai wanted to do business with people who wanted to do business with the Ortega organisation. Quite apart from that, if one of my roles was to think of Nikolai's reputation it wasn't helpful if my own name could be linked, however tangentially, with a Latin drug gang. This was why despite my old contacts – the few who were not by then dead or in jail – I was not involved in the shale initiative; that and my uneasy truce with the DEA.

'In Tamaulipas we sent someone to talk to these people. Rational. Make an offer. They cut off his head.' Though he considered Igor Ortega scarcely more than a jungle savage Nikolai spoke with something like grudging admiration for his negotiating strategy. He glanced at the bodyguard smoking the roll-up, who promptly extinguished it and stood up.

'You're staying tonight?' Nikolai asked. In the morning, he went on, becoming quite animated, we would sail the yacht to Mallorca and see the underground lake at Porto Cristo, before late dinner at Le Caprice in Ibiza. I prepared myself to explain I had to return to London this evening. In turn Nikolai would insist I was mad to contemplate this, though we both knew the propeller plane was waiting and there was no question that in an hour's time I would be sitting in it.

28

5

'Camilla, thank you so much for coming.' I knew Camilla Rhodes-Thorpe took a dim view of me; in fact it was the only thing I really admired about her. 'Is Anders with you?'

During the pause before she answered (Anders was in Shanghai) it occurred that remembering the name of her latest male friend was precisely the sort of tendency of mine she found so objectionable. Camilla was generally seen as a sort of nearly Antonia: beautiful but not enough to appear on the front of *Tatler*; aristocratic (she was an Hon) but not related to royalty. In consequence she resented Antonia even more than the ugly and untitled – if formidably vivacious – Ingy.

Meanwhile the widespread belief that this high society trinity were tremendous friends somehow survived the fact that Ingy and Camilla and Antonia hardly ever occupied the same room – largely because Antonia, with quiet ruthlessness, routinely alternated invitations to her exclusive gatherings between the two other women.

I caught the eye of a girl with a drinks tray. She must have registered my slightly pleading expression because she beat a path through the crowd towards us. 'Have you tried the

English sparkling wine? It's made by a French champagne house who bought a vineyard in Kent. I rather like it.'

Camilla was taking in the lugubrious portraits on the gallery walls for just long enough, I suspected, to reach a conclusive judgement. Absently she plucked a glass from the tray. 'I suppose you would like the idea of a luxury transplant. Though if the grapes are French it seems to me a rather unhappy thing: not *truly* English, but not able to call itself champagne.'

Before I could reply she was on her way back to the octagon, where most of the guests were drinking at a safe remove from the rather mood-killing works we'd gathered to celebrate. In the hope of a few seconds' respite from proceedings I approached one of the paintings. I was examining a spectral face that seemed cocked to one side from the weight of the violently thick paintwork when I saw Roland Turner heading in my direction. The gallery lighting caught the sheen of his high forehead: it made him look like he'd been drinking, though he was usually surprisingly sober for one so intent on causing mischief. I asked if Charlotte, his QC wife, was here.

'She's preparing for a 7 a.m. conference call "with Delhi", as she puts it, as though ten million Indians are feverish for her advice on exploiting double tax relief rules. Now, William, before some terribly annoying person comes up and—'

'I'm not interrupting,' said a thirtysomething woman with a black bob and rather masculine nose. 'So – this is all your fault.'

'Yulia Azarova, this is Roland Turner.' To Roland I explained, 'Yulia is a distinguished interior designer.'

'These pictures would have been perfect for Mallott Hall. I know *exactly* where I would have put them,' she said.

'I should hire you on the spot. My wife is quite brilliant in some ways. For one thing she can fillet a new finance bill faster than a roomful of accountants – that's not a manner of speaking, I've seen her do it. But when it comes to decor she wouldn't know the difference between devising a colour scheme and throwing up on a piece of paper.'

Roland looked dimly on people who brought up absent spouses for any reason except to hold them up for ridicule. That wasn't to say he wasn't quite fond of his wife, though now I thought about it the Turners' ten-million-pound Kensington townhouse didn't lack for white marble and gold circular mirrors and lemon-tart-yellow sofas. I excused myself from the pair, on the (truthful) ground that in Nikolai's absence I'd been asked to say a few words. On the other side of the room I could see a little gathering of Tate people, discreetly waiting to steer me back to the octagon.

'Oh, of course . . .' said Roland reasonably, pressing three fingers to my spine and offering Yulia a dismissive smile most people would have thought better of. As I made my way over to the huddled gallery representatives he explained in a brisk hushed tone that he wanted me to persuade a young man to sign over his struggling family business (luxury luggage items; I realised I owned several myself) to Roland and his capital partners for a knock-down price.

'I've managed to convince the boy to meet me for a drink at the Whig Club tomorrow at six. I'll see you then.'

'Was that all right?'
'The speech? I thought you were charming.'
'I think I hate that word.'

My response surprised us both, though Antonia recovered first. 'Perhaps hating your own talent – I mean really hating it – is part of your charm.' Her smile was not altogether warm. This was partly English unhappiness at having said something almost serious, but I knew she was displeased by my non-appearance at the Claridge's-*Quixote* evening earlier in the week.

'I was sorry to miss dinner the other night, and the opera. I had to go to Spain unexpectedly.'

'There's nothing to apologise for.'

This was said so simply and apparently sincerely that if the speaker were anyone else I'd have believed it without hesitation. 'At any rate, I hope the ants travelled well' – when this cowardly attempt at humour received no response I added, 'I think Camilla disapproves of me.'

'Oh well, Camilla. The other day a woman came up and gave her a weeping embrace, right in the middle of the King's Road. Camilla just stood there frozen. I thought she was being assaulted by a lunatic. It turned out the woman had slept in the bed next to hers for five years; you know, at school. She hadn't the faintest recollection of her existence. So you see.'

'See what?'

'If she has any view on you it's a compliment.'

For a short while neither of us spoke.

'How's Harold?'

'Very well. He has a new passion.'

'Oh yes?'

A lesser woman would have lowered her eyelashes a fraction, or allowed a corner of her mouth to twitch. 'Fifteenth-century market crosses,' Antonia said.

'Ah . . .'

'In fact, I don't think he's said a word to me in over a week.'

'I'm sorry.'

'Don't be,' she shrugged. 'Camilla and Ingy are always telling me how it's a tragic waste Harry doesn't do something with all his learning – write books, I imagine they mean, or give public lectures. But unlike most clever people my husband understands himself perfectly, and in his way he's the happiest person I know.'

'I meant I was sorry for you,' I said, though of course Antonia knew that and blushed.

'Talking of friends, I had a rather strange encounter with one of yours.'

'That must have been tedious.'

'Not at all. He was very – very suave, I suppose, in an unusual sort of way. And such a striking face! There was something a little frightening about it.'

The worst people said of her billionaire husband was that he was frighteningly dull. But if Antonia, whose comportment was otherwise so emulated and admired, had any flaw it was a slight weakness – revealed sparingly, and there in the trace of admiration accompanying her last remark – for faintly insalubrious, even dangerous people. It might have explained my own friendship with her.

'We spoke about Mexico, and specifically your old life there,' Antonia continued. Her eyes were blazing. 'It seems I'm not much of an expert on either subject.'

'What was his name?' I virtually whispered, as if I didn't very well know. Without glancing around I knew there were people circling, wanting the benefit of Antonia's attention. 'And why was he bothering you?'

At that moment we were interrupted by Plum Chilcott, a former royal lady-in-waiting who'd supposedly once broken a paparazzo's leg. There followed a rush of less forthright friends of Antonia's as well as others anxious for me to relay their attendance to Nikolai. By the time I managed to extricate myself, I discovered that for the first time since I'd known her Antonia had left a social event before me.

I'd seen Héctor Comala once in London, last year. The Mexican embassy's Day of the Dead party was a new tradition that had taken unexpected hold; rather like, so I gathered, the British eve of St Patrick's Day dinner in Washington. It was quite possible the same British guests of the Mexican ambassador would have been as aghast at the prospect of a St Patrick's Day celebration as their American counterparts of a *Día de los Muertos* event. As it was, at both parties the enormous quantity of alcohol and reassuring buffer of the Atlantic Ocean seemed to do wonders for everyone's sense of cultural engagement.

Even before spotting Héctor I hadn't planned to stay long. His skin was drawn so tight he might almost have been mistaken for one of the members of the hired band, who'd had their faces painted to resemble skulls – though no member of the band had Héctor's manicured hands, or wore a perfectly fitted Prince of Wales grey flannel suit. I never saw him glance at me but he seemed to glide effort-lessly in my direction. Very soon I could hear him talking with Sir Angus Dorcaster, the former Tory trade minister.

'Have you been yourself?'

Héctor's voice was a deceptively pleasant balance of soft and masculine, American and Spanish. I'd remembered the terrified face of a Sandinista realising to whom – the term 'rendition' had not yet been formalised – he was being delivered. Already by then Héctor had earned himself quite a reputation.

'Been where?' asked Dorcaster.

'Mexico.'

'Never. Well, Cancún once.'

'Cancún is not so interesting.'

'There are worse places, from what I hear.'

When Héctor smiled a pale scar showed itself at his lip. 'I've seen a phrase in the *gringo* papers – please, no offence.'

'None taken.'

' "Mexico descends into violence." This would be interesting news to the Aztecs and Comanches. The *conquistadores* and Zapatistas.'

'No, quite,' said Sir Angus, sounding slightly ruffled – he'd clearly expected a more tourist-board-approved take on Mexican history. 'Your country was never Switzerland. Then again I might expect *The Economist* to focus on the consolidation of drug cartels, say, or the fluctuating price of cocaine.'

'It's not so much about drugs,' I heard Héctor say, matter-of-factly. 'Or maybe not so much as you think. Revenue generation is very diverse these days: extortion, kidnapping, oil-theft, people-trafficking. These are just the illegitimate businesses. We must not forget the most lucrative of all, *la política*.' When I turned to leave I met Héctor's gaze for long enough to see the scar become a thin bar of light.

Needless to say I declined the invitation to this year's Day of the Dead party.

Except for Mrs Belsey, my building in Onslow Square was empty. Or that at any rate was my impression: the overseas owners mostly used their flats as occasional pieds-à-terre and the rest of the time didn't bother getting in tenants. Naturally this suited me well, which was to say that in letting Diana take my spare set of keys my flat was no longer a sanctum, and for this and other reasons I now regretted my impulsive decision. How would I explain it to Nikolai if she returned? If she was waiting in my kitchen for me now, with news that Héctor had paid her a visit? Or that Rafael's headless body had been discovered on a Matamoros roadside?

As I stepped out of the creaking lift I saw that my front door was fractionally ajar. I remembered the care Diana had taken on her last visit, despite her flustered state, to avoid snapping her wine glass stem. In the hallway the air was stale with a sharp note of rust, and in the sitting room the lights were still on. The first thing I noticed was my Kramer knife on the coffee table, the one I'd used to slice a lemon after making up a story about milky tea in Agua Clara. It looked as if the entire object had been dipped in a thin paint and negligently left to dry on the oxblood mahogany.

Beside the sofa was a pooled form. I'd seen dead bodies before, but there was something different about finding one in my Kensington flat, lazily covered by an old Liberty throw I'd had for years. Taking care where I placed my feet I knelt down and slowly drew back the throw, bracing myself for the metallic stench. A pair of skinny jeans, darkened in great blooming patches, bore the label of Guess? – I dully registered the low humour while my gaze travelled to the spoiled cream V-neck and slumbering arrangement of arms. It was Diana, of course. I glanced at her throat. The wound was very recent; the blood hadn't yet started to congeal and I could feel, or believed I could, the residual warmth of her body. From my perspective – monstrous as it was, I had to think in such a manner – this was especially bad news, since it made me chief suspect in a homicide investigation.

Part II

6

Though hardly in the mood, I decided not to cancel my appointment with Roland Turner at the Whig Club. As Ingy Vowles liked to observe I rarely stayed long at social events, but having accepted an invitation to something, however minor or excruciating, I would then almost unfailingly and with brutal punctuality attend. (I sometimes joked this unfashionable habit was down to my strict Lutheran upbringing, and it might have been true.)

Plainly, the appearance of a corpse in my flat made it essential to give the general impression my life was proceeding unremarkably, and this included keeping my diary engagements as dependably as usual. I also hadn't forgotten that Roland had held out the prospect of making some money; the dire state of my finances meant I had little choice but to follow up even such vague opportunities.

Despite its name, the Whig Club did not exude an obviously reformist atmosphere. An Andean-looking boy in a bow tie followed my lips apprehensively – we were both under the appraising eye of his moustachioed boss – as I explained I wasn't a member but here to meet Roland Turner at the bar.

'Mr Turner is on the terrace, sir,' interjected the older man. He invited his apprentice to show me to where Roland was drinking an aperitif, receiving my thanks with an obscurely defiant expression which was perhaps attributable to shyness; that or the rowdy chanting coming in waves down the oval staircase. I followed the South American past terracotta-tiled columns and portraits of eminent foreign secretaries. A number of tables were already occupied in the main dining room. This didn't come as a great surprise – more than once I'd been told that dinner was served at 6 p.m. at the older boarding schools and at Oxbridge colleges. (A visiting Parisian or Roman's disapproval of this unsophisticated habit would have been met by the members with a great deal of self-deprecating agreement without being taken at all seriously.)

The dining room gave way to an open loggia followed by a short flight of descending steps. It was a warm evening and Roland sat alone on the busy terrace, this for him unhappy state unimproved by the nesting bottle of Pol Roger.

'We'll need another flute,' Roland said briskly to my chaperone. 'Actually make it two.'

'Thank you,' I said to the boy, then, noticing his stricken look, added quietly, '*Dos copas más.*'

'I shall inform the waiter!' the boy replied at over-compensating volume.

'You're forgiven then?' Roland said when we were alone.

'Forgiven by whom?'

'For missing the *Quixote* evening.'

'Was it any good?'

'I always think it's one of the more screamingly dull operas, so I'm probably not the man to ask.' He glanced at me with unusual coyness. 'It's not that I'm trying to pry or suggest that there's anything going on between the two of you. I suppose I just mean it's a rather dangerous game; one that's gone wrong before – for others, of course. Never for her.'

Though by no means immune to gossip, Roland didn't at heart take much interest in other people's affairs. I assumed his present concern was that I didn't have some great falling out with Antonia that would make me less useful to Nikolai. 'I'm afraid you've completely lost me,' I lied.

'The first Lady of London. The face that lunched a thousand shits. I suppose that's a reasonable summary of her looks and – if she weren't, in person, so *tasteful* – rather relentless social career. Though I've never quite been convinced Antonia Highclere is as demure as she seems,' Roland mused. 'There's a hidden steeliness; that's what everyone really finds so besotting, even if they don't realise it.' He paused. 'Or not until it's too late.'

Usually she was one of the few people it didn't bore me to think about, but given the personalised tone of the current discussion I was keen to move things on. 'I think you've given me the essential details about the hoped-for luggage company acquisition . . .' I said.

'A family business, rather faded and forgotten these days but popular with various cosmopolitans in the thirties: Lindbergh, Harold and Vita, even Edward VIII apparently. You may have thought no one would be ghastly enough to have strong opinions about a suitcase – or perhaps it's different in America – but despite bleeding money right now the company has significant heritage value, particularly in the Asian markets. The co-investors and new management team are already lined up.'

'Meanwhile the heir is weighing another offer.'

'Dorian Hamilton. His father dropped dead of a heart attack six months ago and the boy inherited the business. An art school moron, though I suppose that's to be expected by the third generation.' Roland glanced at his watch, as if noting the pitiless effluxion of time. 'I'm hoping you'll be able to talk some sense into him. You always sound so . . . what's the word. Plausible.'

'Do you know much about them? The rivals?'

'I know they've doubled my offer!' Roland said, while I watched his spasming unkempt eyebrows. In a more serious tone, he added that the other investors were backed by a Russian fund. His plan, I realised, rested not so much on my own persuasive powers with Dorian Hamilton but those of my patron with his fellow countrymen. My role was to be the silent messenger, the message being the rival buyers should back off. (Nikolai had a reputation for complicating his enemies' lives by means of varying legality across multiple jurisdictions. 'Enemies' were all those who didn't dedicate their lives to his personal enrichment.) Offhandedly, Roland mentioned my half-million or so commission from the exit profit, though it would take a few years to turn the business around before selling it on to the Chinese or Indians. I didn't want to say I couldn't really afford to wait that long, just as Roland didn't want to spell out what he saw as the really key inducement (he had a blessedly vague idea of my finances), namely the advantage of having Roland and his capital partners – a former chairman of the Board of Trade; an entrepreneur friend of Prince Charles; an ancient, now 'boutique' merchant bank – owe Nikolai and, to a lesser extent, me their gratitude.

'One thing I forgot to mention,' Roland said, looking expectantly past my shoulder. 'The boy is half-American. Half Asian-American, in fact; his mother's mother was born in Manila, which I suppose makes him quarter Filipino. Anyway, probably best not to dwell on it.' Rising to welcome his guest, he added through a rapturous grin, 'The parents divorced when he was young, and the mother lives in San Diego. As far as I can tell she has no involvement with the business.'

It wasn't until after Roland had left, claiming a dinner appointment and with the bill for a pair of empty bottles of Pol Roger unpaid, that I heard the boy say more than two words together. Having secured us fresh drinks from the bar – not strictly necessary, given the attentive table service, but I felt the need to gather my spirits – I began by suggesting that San Diego must have been a wonderful place to grow up, at least partially.

Dorian took a sip of Negroni, winced, and then drank half of it down. 'It's true I'm famously immature.'

'I meant because you were also educated in this country.'

'My father thought there were too many Mexicans. Too many *Filipinos*, for that matter.'

'And what do you think?'

'I suppose I prefer London,' Dorian said with a shrug. 'At least here people care about artists.'

I didn't think he should get carried away with that thought. (Roland had earlier announced, the reflexive boastfulness of his tone belying his indifference, that Dorian was interested in 'collage art'.)

Changing the subject, I said, 'It's rough to lose a parent when you're young. I'm sorry.'

His face went very still. He had high cheekbones and a light complexion which was implausibly smooth, except for two deep grooves when he smiled. Back at the club the first thing I'd noticed about his physical aspect was his limp: one of his knees seemed about to buckle every time he put weight on it.

Looking intently at me, he said, 'Roland mentioned you were half-American.'

'On my father's side, but I never lived there.'

'You don't have the accent.'

'Nor you,' I said – another lie.

His smile revealed perfect teeth, so white they were almost blue. 'They beat it out of me.'

I remarked that boarding school can't have been much fun.

'It wasn't all bad,' said Dorian, gazing with self-conscious mistiness at the bronze chandelier. He wore an aftershave which was just then being publicised on the side of almost every double-decker bus, and which didn't truthfully add to any sense of mystique he was trying to cultivate.

'When I was at school – this was in Paris, or just outside – one of the older boys took exception to my eyes.'

'What was wrong with them?' he indignantly demanded.

'Too large. When we were in the same room I was obliged to shut them and face the wall.'

'But you have *wonderful* eyes! They're sort of Californian, actually. Like a Hockney swimming pool.' Then Dorian caught himself, and took a sulky sip of Negroni. 'Just so you know I'm not stupid. I know Roland has put you up to this.'

'Put me up to what?'

'Persuading me to sell him the family company.'

'Of course you're right,' I said. 'Though he's not paying for this meal, in case you were thinking of getting your revenge via the wine list.'

He saw I wasn't joking, or not entirely, and broke into a grin. 'What was the name of this school?' he said abruptly.

'Saint Valentin.'

'And the town? You said it was outside Paris.'

'Cergy-Pontoise.' As if there'd been no subtext to his question, I began to describe life in a French boarding school. (I didn't want him to feel humiliated or obliged to admit he didn't know whether there was any such place as Cergy-Pontoise, which rendered his sleuthing rather pointless.) The account owed a certain debt to *Lacombe, Lucien* and later, for a whimsical escapade involving a dilapidated nearby chateau, *Le Grand Meaulnes*. Dorian's gaze had drifted to a spot beneath my shoulder. Rather than pay attention to my increasingly reckless narrative he was turning over some private matter in his mind. I began to regret how little of a challenge the young man seemed capable of offering, if only because it meant there was nothing to stop my own thoughts from sliding.

Nikolai's people had removed Diana's body, along with the Kramer knife and soiled oriental rug and Liberty throw. Naturally, I was grateful for their assistance – though I was given no information on their plans for these objects and it was disconcerting to have no choice but to trust in their competence. I was also unsure where all this left me with the Russian himself. All day I'd waited for a car to arrive to pick me up, but none came, and nor did my landline ring.

Regardless of the warmth or otherwise of Nikolai's present feelings towards me, I needed urgently to speak with him about Héctor Comala. Two things seemed reasonably clear in relation to the Mexican diplomat. The first was that his cartel paymasters had been weakened since the fatal shooting last year of Nicolas José, the elder and saner Ortega sibling, ostensibly by the federal police. (In fact the orders were rumoured to have come from within the cartel itself, specifically younger brother Igor.) This explained Rafael Domínguez Saavedra's apparent decision to steal from them, as well as the recent upsurge in violence in Tamaulipas – not to mention Héctor's banishment from the Policía Federal Ministerial to 'political liaison' at the London embassy. Rival narco empires and, just as dangerously, the Mexican state, which tended to align itself with whichever cartel held the most power, must have smelt blood.

Secondly, Héctor was quite capable of following Diana to my flat and cutting her throat on his own initiative, not just for the pleasure of tormenting me but also to curry favour with the out-of-sorts cartel. Without overstating his intellectual resources, Igor Ortega's opposition to the idea of surviving relatives bordered on the philosophical. What was more he'd probably relish displaying the cartel's extra-territorial reach, particularly if they hadn't yet hunted down Rafael. In short, Héctor and Igor were different species of psychopath, and it was my bad luck that even by moving continents I wasn't free of them.

'I'm going to a party tonight,' Dorian interrupted during my story of midnight revelry at the mysterious chateau. 'It should be pretty wild.'

7

We weren't in a chateau but a former meat storage building somewhere east. 'At least take that off!' Dorian shouted of my tie, which like all my ties I'd acquired at Charvet in Paris. I ignored his advice. If one was going to be overdressed it felt better to be emphatic about it, a little in the same way that William Strunk, of *The Elements of Style*, advised his students that if they were unsure how to pronounce a word they should say it especially loudly.

A lift took us up to the first floor. Initially I thought we'd arrived at an art gallery. A vast space with whitewashed walls, onto one of which *Roma città aperta* was being projected. (Or *Rome, Open City*: I'd learned that in England it was rarely acceptable to use foreign words if one could help it. I hadn't forgotten Antonia's faintly horrified smile when an American once asked her if she'd care for *gelato*.) Such furniture as there was looked as though it had been retrieved from a skip earlier in the evening and arranged haphazardly. As a further gesture to ambience, the overhead strip lighting had been switched off and replaced with a profusion of candles, so that the whole place was a casual arm-swipe away from a massacre.

But the key feature of the commune, or whatever it was, was the young people. A man in his early twenties and dressed in a Strunkian evening jacket supplied me with a Martini before asking my views on General el-Sisi. I wondered if he'd mistaken me for a Middle Eastern scholar he'd been chatting with minutes earlier, or if he was working from some eccentric manual for interacting with fifty-somethings. He took in my reply with an expression of intense concentration, though I noticed he was listing at a rather unnatural angle.

Everyone had mysterious jobs. They usually involved the Internet in some form or other and were so abstract-sounding I started to feel better about my own rather hazy occupation. They were well travelled in the literal sense – they liked to list where they'd been and were going next, Marrakesh or Venice or Berlin. On the other hand they had little confidence in their grasp of Western history and culture. A girl with a razor-straight fringe and wrist tattoo was scandalised and perhaps slightly titillated when I replied I was not myself a great admirer of Rossellini, and (when she pressed me further) said I tried not to add failures of pacing in works of art to my own deficiencies, numerous as these were.

It became clear that those who knew Dorian were under the false impression he was enormously rich. Thanks to Roland, I of course already knew the truth about the boy's finances, though from my own experience I was aware how this sort of misconception could arise when one had a habit of spending a great deal of money. Probably Dorian had received a sizeable allowance while his father was alive and was now drawing a large salary from the struggling family company. He didn't strike me as having much of a head for numbers, so it was possible he had only a vague idea of the business's near insolvency. Nor (from my casual questioning over dinner) did he appear to have much sentimental interest in the history of Hamilton Luggage, or for that matter hard-headed curiosity about the world of commerce. This suggested he would simply divest the enterprise to the highest seller, whereas to earn my commission from Roland I had to convince Dorian not to act in strict conformity with his interests. And I had to do this without playing my trump card of mentioning Nikolai – who wouldn't thank me for involving him in such a trivial matter, especially given the present delicacy of our relations – to either the rival investors or Dorian.

At some point I realised I'd lost sight of the boy himself. I made my way up to the roof of the building. Half-a-dozen inflatable hot-tubs had been set up, and bathers were lolling in groups. Beyond them was a concrete wasteland, a drab gasworks; further off the City and Canary Wharf glittered like Sodom and Gomorrah.

'*There* you are!' called a voice behind me. When I turned round I saw Dorian commence limping towards me. He did so without any word of departure to the person he'd been talking to, a shaven-headed fellow whose row of black earrings, curved and sharp at their tips, resembled the nails of a dog. 'Let's go back downstairs,' Dorian said. His eyes were not quite in focus, and he seemed slightly relieved to have found me. 'I want you to meet my friend Edwin. He's a genius, literally – he has an IQ of 180.'

'That sounds quite a burden.'

'You've no idea. He can't do a normal job with a brain that size, though of course the government welfare people don't understand so he's basically homeless. Well, technically he's heir to half of Scotland, only he doesn't get on with his father. He gets terribly depressed about it all.'

'In much wisdom,' I said, 'is much grief.'

I caught a flash of Dorian's dazzling teeth. 'That's from the Bible! Must be your American side.'

On the subject of body parts I asked what had happened to his knee. Had Dorian been completely English I wouldn't have risked such a personal question. As it was he didn't seem at all offended. 'The old hop-along thing? I had cancer in my knee when I was a kid. The operation . . .' At that moment we were obliged to push through a crowd of bodies by the rooftop entrance, but perhaps he saw no need to finish the sentence.

I followed Dorian as he hobbled down the narrow stairwell and then along a maze of corridors leading off the main communal space, which was by now almost unbearably hot from the candles and general crush of young people. Finally we reached a drab little bedroom. Inside, a tall figure, Edwin presumably, lounged on the narrow bed, while a handful of acolytes of both sexes hugged their knees or lay sprawled on the concrete floor. Everyone's eyes were glazed but the room smelled of nothing in particular, apart from perhaps a faint tang of post-adolescent sweat. I already felt a certain wariness towards a genius who made a note of his IQ score and was not above letting this slip to his more impressionable friends.

'The mysterious *consigliere*,' Edwin said, after giving me the briefest of glances. 'I hope you're not planning to take advantage of poor Dorry. But if you are, you should know that while he might be on the dim side' – protesting at the tittering, Dorian sounded exaggeratedly American – 'he's not actually mentally defective.'

'I think perhaps you're confused,' I said.

'About what?'

'Me.'

He pushed a lock of grease-darkened hair from his eyes. With his delicate ashen face he looked like a handsomely ailing tsarevich. 'Why should Dorry sell his family company for half what the Russian lot are offering?'

'It's true that our offer is structured so that he'd receive less upfront. But we'll do a better job of reminding people of the company's history.' I was uncomfortable discussing this publicly, but Dorian clearly put great store by his friend's opinions and I had little choice but to play along.

I said, 'When we eventually sell it on, Dorian stands to make much more than under the other offer.' This was an improvisation. I didn't know if he stood to receive any further payment out of the eventual sell-on profit; in fact it was rather unlikely.

'Why should anyone believe that?'

'It's what Roland Turner does. He puts his own money at stake – and he's very rich.'

'Will *you* be involved?' Dorian asked hesitantly.

I made sure to meet the boy's eye. 'That's something we could discuss.'

To pre-empt anyone going further into a topic that was evidently starting to bore him, Edwin asked Dorian if he'd brought 'the package'. After a moment's confusion, Dorian with proud solemnity handed over a little vacuum-sealed bag from his velvet jacket pocket. At the sight of this Edwin sprang to life. He reached down and fetched a roll of aluminium foil from beneath the bed, before tearing off a strip which he gave to a brown-haired girl. Next he tapped out a sizeable amount of powder onto the foil. He took out a small glass pipe from his pocket, which he handed to me.

'For God's sake be careful!' said another girl who had been reclining on her elbow like a mermaid on a rock, and now sat up. 'That's white heroin. Someone died injecting it in Amsterdam last week.'

'The man wants Dorry to take a risk,' Edwin said in a measured tone, as if the logic of the scene spoke for itself.

With a hint of a sneer the brown-haired girl said, 'Ready?' Like any good assistant, she knew to let the moment stretch before clicking the lighter. A smell of burnt syrup filled the little room as I chased the trails of smoke.

When at some point Edwin spoke again he seemed to shimmer with satisfaction. 'I know who you are. You're William Hoffer. I once heard you discussed by an American journalist – some London bureau chief,' he said in a tone that implied he knew several. Perhaps he did.

'Where was this?' My voice was gratifyingly normal.

'At one of my parents' parties. She said the rumour was you were kicked out of West Point after a terrible scandal. Then you were some sort of CIA double agent in the eighties, lurking around in Cuba and Central America. Now you work for Russian oligarchs. She thought you were probably managing their money in return for a commission. No one has ever caught you doing anything illegal, at least' – smirking – 'not until a few seconds ago, and you have some powerful friends. So for the moment your secrets are safe.'

He held out his hand and the mermaid girl passed him a silver vaporiser. In my confused state I mistook it for a bullet, one of the old Winchester .30-30 hunting cartridges. He let it dangle between his slender fingers, watching me closely, before taking a deep puff. 'I think what really surprises everyone is how a farmhand from Ohio ended up so refined. What did it cost you to acquire that accent?' He leaned forward. 'What did it cost someone else?'

'I can't believe you did that. Fuck!' Dorian said in the taxi. He was drunk, his head now and then lolling against my shoulder as I stared at the murky outline of Regent's Park. 'Was it true what Edwin was saying about you?'

'What part?' I said without looking at him.

'The stuff about being a spy and working for gangsters.'

The taxi arrived at Dorian's flat in Little Venice. He got out the car somewhat reluctantly. I was relieved I'd remembered to call Agustina yesterday morning and tell her to take the day off – I didn't plan on rising until well after noon.

Dorian made a circling gesture with his fist. I wound the passenger window down.

'*Was* it true?' he asked.

'You said yourself your friend was mentally defective.'

As the taxi drew away I caught a glimpse of the boy's crushed expression. It was only then I remembered it was in fact Edwin who'd made the remark about Dorian (or rather that he *wasn't* mentally defective), meaning I might have undone the entire evening's work.

8

Around 7 a.m. – I hadn't slept – I made coffee. While New Zealand thermal mud dried on my face I picked up a book from my bedside table. It was a biography of Joseph Duveen, son of provincial Dutch Jews, who died Lord Duveen of Millbank having made a fortune selling old masters to Gilded Age industrialists. I skimmed the pages until I could rinse off the mud and examine myself: a touch grey, perhaps, but more or less acceptable in the circumstances. I put on a freshly starched shirt, herringbone silk Charvet tie and Savile Row tweed suit. Finally, to sharpen my mental alertness I swallowed four capsules of modafinil.

Kensington was bathed in sunshine – it felt like the start of a heatwave. On reaching the High Street I stepped inside an old-fashioned red telephone box. I picked up the handset and inserted a coin into the slot, then another and another until the first of two columns of money had vanished. Carefully, from memory, I dialled a long distance number. Following a brief conversation in Spanish I hung up and returned the unused coins to my pocket.

Rafael Domínguez Saavedra was indeed missing. Vigorous enquiries ('*Dicen que Igor está furioso*') had been made by the Ortega cartel regarding his whereabouts.

According to rumour the fool had, as I'd suspected, stolen cartel money – probably not all that much considering the price he was going to pay.

In retrospect I should have confirmed this mix of fact and informed supposition immediately after Diana first showed up at my flat. If I hadn't it was because, though I trusted my old contact as far as it went, by making the call I was implicated further in the mess Rafael had created.

More than ever I needed to speak to Nikolai. I realised I dreaded his displeasure about my situation less than I did Héctor's next move.

On the way home I stopped by the newsagents, where I chatted with the Bombay-born shopkeeper about the upcoming Test match between England and Sri Lanka at Lord's. He spoke loftily about both teams. England's recent victory over India in India – the first in decades – had not shaken his faith in his native country's cricketing superiority, particularly the batting line-up. I was less convinced about the strength of their middle-order since Tendulkar's retirement, but was pleased he seemed not to pay any attention when I laid the *Telegraph* and *Mail* on the counter as well as my usual *Financial Times*.

Back at the flat I made a pot of lapsang souchong before carefully scanning each newspaper for mention of a missing Mexican schoolgirl. To my relief – it was surely only a temporary reprieve – there was nothing.

An hour or so later I was leaving Onslow Square again. This time I wandered as far as Fulham Road before stopping, with the sun warming my face, to hail a cab.

In the hushed lamplit foyer of the offices of Nikolai's investment company I contemplated the Shishkins I'd chosen, a series of lush forest landscapes, which had collectively doubled in value in the last decade. When this satisfying thought began to pale (in the short term the situation in Ukraine would almost certainly compromise the paintings' value), I reread the *FT* from cover to cover.

At last Maksim, one of Nikolai's assistants, appeared. He was thin-faced, barely out of his twenties but already bald apart from a few slightly maddening wisps. The sense that his appearance would remain essentially unchanged for the next thirty years perhaps unfairly contributed to a more general impression of complacency. He was also too junior to know anything useful. I'd half-expected if not the man himself then a phalanx of lawyers and security consultants.

'William! So sorry to make you wait.' He made a vague gesture with his arm, as if to suggest poor timekeeping was as inevitable here as Shishkins or waif-like receptionists, even though on my previous visits someone had always come to fetch me immediately.

'Is he in?' I said, without bothering to say hello. My manners became more Russian in the presence of Max, perhaps because he so frequently played up his Eton schooling, where he'd no doubt learned about Sisyphus and Tantalus: the Greek idea of hell as the denial of what we most want.

'I'm afraid not. If you'd called Frances first you might have spared yourself the journey. Or emailed – I can never remember which you don't use.'

I suggested we find an office.

'Of course,' he said, after a slight pause.

The conference room was rather overwhelmed by the smell of fresh lilacs. I did my best to ignore a Jeff Koons marble bust in the corner, whose acquisition I occasionally worried visitors might think I had something to do with.

Feeling suddenly very tired I said I needed to speak to Nikolai. The matter was important.

'I'm afraid that won't be possible.' Having smugly unburdened himself of this news, he almost immediately gave up that Nikolai was in Thailand. The yacht was on its way to Phuket.

'You're not sailing it through the Gulf of Aden?'

'Most of the crew are ex-Russian army,' he said. 'Quite frankly I'd be more worried about the pirates.'

'I don't care about the *crew*. There's a fifteen-million-pound collection of art on that yacht.'

'No, all the art's being flown out separately.' Max furnished me with a broad smile. 'You see we have everything under control.'

Membership of the gym near Nikolai's offices was so rarely sought by someone whose fees weren't covered by one of the neighbouring hedge funds, the manager had been obliged to come up with a rate specifically for me. Despite the exorbitant cost I felt it was a useful social investment.

Just now, however, it served as a place to think without interruption. My limbs felt achy and leaden as I made myself complete a hundred lengths in the underground pool, glimpsing at alternate strokes and without interest the images of the Great Barrier Reef projected on an opaque glass screen.

Afterwards I didn't see anyone I knew in the changing room. The two men closest to me were discussing their triathlon training regimes; they were about my age or slightly younger. When one of them left, the unfinished conversation hung in the air. The remaining chap smiled at me with an air of innocent sociability – I was bound to be the right sort, everyone here was. Even though he probably managed a billion-pound fund, and was exactly the type I usually came here to meet, I was surprised to find myself doubting my ability to maintain the simplest exchange. Before long he joined another discussion.

It was coming up to lunchtime. I hadn't eaten in over twenty-four hours, since before the Tate party. It was not unusual for me to miss consecutive meals – last night, some-what to my relief, Dorian had dismissed the idea of inter-rupting our drinking for dinner – but my appetite still showed no sign of returning, so I wandered towards Bond Street, where my mood was instantly lifted by the proxim-ity of objects of vertu. In the third gallery I visited, near Sotheby's, a rather distinguished miniature bronze skeleton took my eye.

'The memento mori belonged to Pierre and Yves,' said the discreet presence appearing at my shoulder. 'Pierre Bergé and Yves Saint Laurent,' the dealer added with a plummy flourish when I didn't respond.

'Yes, I thought it might have,' I said, hoping my casual tone would discourage him from doubling the price. I had just enough of an idea about seventeenth-century figures from the Augsburg workshop to know I couldn't really afford one – the worst sort of buyer, in other words – and I gave the dealer a strange pitying smile when finally, having idly but at some length inspected a Hispano-Philippine carved ivory head of Christ and a silk Tibetan thangka, I was ready to start negotiations.

Half-an-hour later I was mired in thoughts of Nikolai's sudden and ominously un-signalled (to me) exit from the country when I bumped into Gianni Bardoni, the auctioneer. He was leaving the Nicholas Lyle gallery.

'Guglielmo,' he said, kissing me on each cheek. 'I was just wondering who I was going to lunch with.' The sense he was taunting me with those words was confirmed when he added, closing his eyes with pleasure, 'Do you *lunch*, Guglielmo?'

'I *have* lunch' – Gianni liked to create comic identities for his friends and mine was that I was correct. 'But I'm afraid I don't have long,' I protested vaguely, since I knew I'd end up paying.

'Nonsense! For one thing you don't have a job. But as it happens I have a busy afternoon, so we'll need to confine ourselves to somewhere simple.'

'Any ideas?'

Gianni was gripping my arm as though the mental strain of choosing might cause him to collapse. In the end I felt only a faint slump when he conceded there was always Le Gavroche.

Shortly after we sat down Gianni observed, leaving the impression the statements might be obscurely linked, that the house champagne was not a complete disaster and that Sir What's-his-name was at the next table.

'What is it they call him?'

'Father of the House.'

'I wonder if they'll ever have a Mother,' he said, scanning the menu. 'That's what those naughty politicians really want. *Ras-el-Hanout fenouil* sounds like something one would find in a Marseille street market.'

'Actually—'

'I do find it irritating how the French insist on writing everything in French – Italian restaurants in London are never so presumptuous.'

I assumed he wasn't being serious but one could never quite tell. The waiter, Emmanuel, greeted us both like old friends, which since Gianni and I had never eaten together at this restaurant before caused us to swap jealous glances for no reason in particular, certainly on my part. Emmanuel presumably knew the coming exchange was going to feel like an interrogation by some august public prosecutor. (It was not impossible the grey at Gianni's temples had been phased back in for just these occasions.) The proceedings went on for so long it came as a surprise when at last, with every line of the menu raked over to the Italian's satisfaction, and with a £400 bottle of Sassicaia to my quiet alarm on its way, the Italian turned to me and announced he had better earn his crust before the wine arrived. 'The middle market for Russian art has already gone,' he was soon saying. 'If the beefcake in the Kremlin keeps this up the masterpieces will be next.'

I tried not to think about the Shishkins.

'Which means we'll have to find another way of steering the Comrades past Koons.'

'*Il faut vouloir rêver et savoir rêver*,' I said, wondering if his new objection to French extended to Baudelaire.

'Well, quite. And despite your best efforts, my dear William, one finds plenty of *vouloir* and not much *savoir*. Though I suppose it took the Greeks a generation or two to get the hang of things.'

A young waitress arrived – perhaps Emmanuel's courage had failed him – with two foie gras mousses.

I said, 'This morning I came across an old story about a rich Californian industrialist who wanted to start an art collection. His friend had secured him an appointment with Joseph Duveen.'

'At the Ministry of Marine, I suppose.'

'When the Californian spotted a Rembrandt and made enquiries about buying it, Duveen assured him he couldn't possibly sell such a work to a man who owned no paintings.'

'I'm afraid the time when the worst thing one could do to great art was sell it to Americans is long gone,' he said. 'But no one knows that more than you. Ah, at last! *Arriva il vino*.'

In the course of the third bottle of wine – Gianni's busy afternoon had received no further mention – I was reflecting on the entente between the Frenchness of the restaurant (food and menus and staff) and the soothing English clubbishness of the patterned carpet and House-of-Commons-green walls.

'. . . That's the thing about lunch with you,' said Gianni, clutching his wine glass nurturingly to his chest. 'On the one hand it's slightly dull, because you're so discreet. But for a Catholic there's something wonderfully nostalgic about it.'

'I was actually close to that once. Becoming a man of the cloth.'

'Hmm? Yes, precisely,' Gianni said, who'd abandoned any pretence of listening to me. Soon he was complaining about recently having to entertain Chinese clients the auction house had flown over. ('They wanted me to show them a *casino*. My dear, I hold a doctorate on della Robbia!')

At the best of times I found it an effort to talk to almost anyone for longer than an hour or so – though of course I regularly did; it was a matter of discipline and routine, like swimming lengths. This desire to be alone was not particularly about preferring my own company; after all, one's self-awareness was at its most agreeably faint without the differentiating presence of other people. On the whole human beings interested me well enough. I simply would have preferred no returning gaze forcing shape and form on me – to be free to take them in as if they were pieces of art.

Back at Onslow Square, I opened my garret windows and positioned the squat Chippendale chair to catch the last of the afternoon sun. To keep awake I turned up *La bohème* and drank briny Martinis with far more vermouth than Gianni would have tolerated. I tried in vain not to think of the money I'd spent on the little bronze skeleton – itself an attempted distraction from the probably wasted evening with Dorian – or the object's larger morbid theme. I drifted in and out of sleep as penniless Rodolfo sang of giving up Mimi. In the shadows of the room, Nikolai and Diana and Héctor had begun dancing like grotesque Day of the Dead celebrants.

9

Merely acknowledging the array of galleries inside the V&A – more than a hundred spread over six levels – required a certain gathering of spirits. From the Cromwell Road entrance I turned left down a long corridor, where I passed a panel of Ottoman tiles not unlike those in Antonia's kitchen, followed by a calming row of Buddhas. Guarding the Raphael cartoons gallery was a fierce Shiva mask with coiled snakes for earrings and little skulls embedded in the crown.

I remained at a loose end. My activities for Nikolai, and more importantly a plan for dealing with Héctor Comala, were at best in limbo until the Russian's return from the Far East. Most likely my patron had lost enthusiasm for me, ever since he was forced to choose between intervening in my situation and sooner or later becoming dragged into a police investigation into the murder of a teenage girl.

The political backdrop – Russia's annexation of the Crimea and her support for Ukrainian separatists – was a further complication. The president's unpredictability was something Nikolai priced without discussion into all his thinking, in the same way that he never referred directly to the basis of his good relations with the Kremlin, namely his (Nikolai's) self-imposed exile. I didn't need to be told of the ever-increasing importance Nikolai attached to maintaining his British safe harbour, and with it his good standing here; nor that complicating his plans – however unwittingly – was deeply unwise.

The lighting in the Raphael room was soothingly low. Two vast metallic sails, a contemporary art installation, were suspended from the ceiling. They rotated at times together and at others in opposing directions; their reflective surfaces made the room appear to float and sway in dreamlike fashion.

Though I had come here to see the hanging structures, the room itself, with its permanent collection of biblical-themed tapestries and gilded altarpiece, resembled the sort of consecrated space I usually avoided. It was why despite the Vasari quotation on the wall declaring Raphael a mortal god I felt only muted admiration for the large-scale canvas designs showing familiar scenes: the miraculous catch of fish, Peter and John healing a cripple, Christ addressing the disciples. Of more obvious dramatic interest was *The Death of Ananias*. It was hard not to feel some sympathy for the man felled by Saint Peter for the sin of withholding a small part of the proceeds of selling his land. The skin over Ananias's cartoonishly muscled body was reptilian green, the same colour as the gown of his penny-counting wife, who would shortly be struck dead like her husband.

I came last to the fifteenth-century Spanish altarpiece. Already standing before it was a short jowly man about my age in a crumpled off-the-peg suit. The first impression he left was innocuous, even forgettable. But I had a good memory for faces, and a slight chill came over me on realising I'd already seen the man once this morning, hovering around the entrance to the arcade at South Kensington tube station.

In this somewhat perturbed state I tried to take in the altarpiece. Its lower half was taken up with a depiction of Saint George slaying the dragon. On either side of this a series of panels showed various martyrdoms of the warrior saint: Sant Jordi, in the Catalan account, being dragged by horses and boiled in a cauldron and beheaded. At the centre of the altarpiece a Christian army vanquished the Moors. Above were more peaceful images – the Madonna and Child; George rescuing a virgin princess from the dragon – but by then I was starting to feel slightly dizzied by the whirring sails overhead, and had seen enough.

'I'll just join you for a moment.' Ingy Vowles said this with an uncharacteristic note of hesitance, making me fear it was obvious how little I welcomed her arrival – indeed how much like a harpy she appeared to me in that moment.

I was sitting at a table outside the Comptoir Libanais, ostensibly reading the *FT*. (I'd already scoured the other papers in the privacy of my flat and found no mention of Diana.) In fact I'd been pondering two particular problems. Assuming Diana had brought a mobile phone with her on her initial visit to my flat, the police – perhaps among others – would be able to establish via the device's satellite data that she had been in Onslow Square that evening.

And of course there was a witness to confirm this, in the form of Mrs Belsey. If or when Diana's disappearance surfaced in the news, the octogenarian would undoubtedly recognise my 'goddaughter' to whom she had lent her spare keys.

My new companion declared we might as well celebrate the approach of midday (it was half past ten) with a bottle of Prosecco. I was about to order a second coffee, having resolved to have a dry day, but it would have been ungallant not to join her.

'How are you, Ingy?'

'Oh, *I'm* fine.'

I was immediately on guard. 'And Julian?'

'Julian? Same as always. He was moaning this morning about having to go to parliament. I told him I'd never heard of the Treasury Select Committee, and anyway they no longer hang people outside Westminster Hall.'

Ingy hadn't removed her sunglasses. These were so dramatically oversized she claimed a man had once, on one of the rare occasions she left Kensington, offered her his arm to cross the road. She'd lamented afterwards if only the handsome Frenchmen of her own borough were so easily confused by Dior.

The way the light caught the waxy marks on her cheek made me think of Héctor's lip, with its narrow column of scar tissue. Like much else about him its cause was unknown or at least not public knowledge. A commonplace cantina scuffle, perhaps; it was not hard to imagine a boozed-up vaquero coming at the scrawny Indian with the fathomlessly superior smile, though doubtless it wouldn't have finished well for the vaquero.

When the Prosecco arrived Ingy toasted me with discomforting zeal. 'Well, what's your news?' she asked, perhaps wanting to prolong the suspense.

I mentioned my visit earlier that morning to see the installation in the Raphael room. This bored her but she knew she ought to keep vaguely abreast of cultural happenings and that I was sensible enough not to linger on them unnecessarily. Of my lunch with Gianni Bardoni, I relayed his withering account of accompanying Chinese gamblers to ever-ghastlier West End casinos, but held back from mentioning details of the auction house's financial difficulties, which he'd divulged over his second or third vin santo. Ingy would have found this more interesting at the cost of weakening her faith in my discretion.

'I do love the way you tell stories, William. You never make too much of them.'

'I think you're having fun with me.'

'Not at all!' She gulped her Prosecco. 'Or maybe a little. I was just thinking about Antonia. How her great skill is discovering slightly unlikely people.'

I smiled.

'Don't take that the wrong way. I'm saying you're a triumph. It's her great accomplishment – *you're* her great accomplishment – much more than being distantly related to the Windsors, or the modelling thing.'

'I happened to visit the National Portrait Gallery recently,' I said. 'I didn't realise Antonia was there.'

'No, well. It's not the sort of thing she'd mention.'

Nor her friends, I thought. It didn't surprise me that Ingy, with her tormented skin, was not eager to dwell on

Antonia's beauty. 'I think it was Mario Testino,' I said, 'sometime in the nineties.'

'I suppose it's a bit like the fashion business – Antonia's world these days, I mean. The constant demand for novelty.' Ingy paused. 'She's never had money, you know, thanks to her disastrous drunk of a brother; just the title. People often make the mistake of forgetting that about her.'

'Perhaps it's more that they remember Harold's diamond fortune.'

'William, don't be tiresomely literal! I'm not saying Antonia isn't *rich*, at least in theory. You know perfectly well what Harold is like, how madly opposed he is to the most trivial expenditure.'

'But the modelling . . .'

'She never did it for that long, despite how famous it seems to have made her. Anyway, she spent all her earnings years ago.'

Her phone rang and I waited while she made plans for lunch at Scott's. Usually I enjoyed studying Ingy, the way she distinguished between certain types of bad manners. Asking someone what they did for a job at a dinner party, like the unfortunate Luxembourg countess, was gracelessly arriviste not to mention insensitive towards those who didn't work. But ignoring a mobile phone call when one needed to confirm an arrangement would have been prudish and bourgeois, and this was a more delicate matter for Ingy. Despite the U accent and great friendship with Lady Antonia Highclere I would have bet my savings, if I had any, that she came from a long line of Stockholm merchants.

'We were saying something,' she said, having abruptly ended her call.

'The shock of the new.'

'You weren't going to be a protégé forever, William; not at your age. It's because we're friends I can say this to you.'

'No, of course. You think there's a new protégé, as you put it, on the scene.' It was little consolation that Ingy had no idea of the implications of her words.

'He's *Mexican*,' she said wondrously. 'Not even the ambassador! But she'll probably see him again at the Cartier thing, and decide he's a disappointment after all.'

'Cartier? Do you mean the polo?'

'Far more interesting than that. The Foundation is organising a viewing of María Félix's jewellery at the Mexican ambassador's home. It's really just an excuse for a party in Belgrave Square. You knew her, I suppose – in the eighties?'

'María Félix? No, not at all.'

'Well, but you must have met her at least?'

I finished my Prosecco; Ingy waived away my offer of a top-up. 'I saw her at a party in Cuernavaca once. She was surrounded by lots of people.'

'One would hope so,' Ingy said dryly – and it *was* an obvious remark. I sensed she was waiting for some more authenticating detail.

'I'm afraid that's more or less all I remember. She arrived with a Polish friend. I think I chatted with him for a while.'

'You mean you went to a dull gathering in some poky town in Mexico—'

'It's really quite a large city—'

'Somehow, there among the swathes of third world provincials, is a legend of the silver screen—'

'She lived nearby. Her attendance wasn't unexpected—'

'And instead of elbowing your way into her presence you chat politely with the toy boy. To cap it all, this is the version of events you actually tell people.' Ingy at last removed her sunglasses. Her eyes in daylight were like hard gin-soaked olives. 'And you wonder why Antonia finds you hard to replace!' Then, 'Or perhaps you don't.'

I said I should be getting back to Onslow Square. Of course I'd take care of the bill.

'Yes, rough news about Judy Belsey,' she said seamlessly.

'Mrs Belsey?'

A familiar jowly figure, the same man from the South Ken arcade and then the V&A, had just sat down at a nearby table. He began scrutinising the menu as if it were draft legislation.

'A heart attack – in the bookshop.' Ingy gestured in the direction of Thurloe Street. 'I assumed you'd heard.'

'When was this?'

'Yesterday.'

'How awful, I must visit her.'

'It was only a minor thing. Besides, you know Judy: from what I gather they practically had to chloroform her to get her in the ambulance.'

'Which hospital is it?'

'The Chelsea and Westminster – but I should wait until tomorrow, or perhaps Monday. They're doing lots of tests, and anyway her awful glum daughter, Annabel or something, is there now with the grandchildren.'

'I suppose she can still speak?' I asked cautiously. I couldn't quite believe my luck might extend to Mrs Belsey being struck mute. 'Because of the previous stroke, I mean.'

Ingy gripped her Longchamp handbag – her arms were ferociously toned. 'Really, she's *fine*. I didn't know you were so sentimental.'

10

Whatever my worries about the Mexican teenager murdered in my flat, my soon-to-be suspicious landlady, my absent and probably furious Russian patron, my unidentified jowly follower around Kensington, and above all the violent spectre of Héctor Comala, the more mundane problem of my lack of funds had not disappeared. Since I needed rather urgently to drum up some business, and had recently and at great expense renewed my Centre Court debenture, after lunch I decided to go to Wimbledon.

Opening Mondays had been fruitful in the past: even experienced types could become slightly giddy with anticipation of the tennis, especially if the weather was good and you made sure they had plenty to drink. The last few years – ever since I'd been working more or less exclusively for Nikolai – I came simply to watch the matches, often accompanying Antonia, who was passionate about the championships though somehow not in a way that felt relentless or exhausting.

Almost immediately on entering the All England Club I found myself ducking into a merchandise shop. I'd spotted an investment manager acquaintance, his face a ghastly leer as he recounted some anecdote or other to his beer-flushed companion. Despite my evasive action, the truth was that the same people whom today I'd ingratiatingly be sounding out for work I might not have so much as acknowledged twelve months ago. Thus while part of me hoped I'd run into Antonia at some point, I knew if it happened there was a strong risk of humiliation.

As for my unhappy finances: I was too cowardly, and possibly too lazy, to grapple with vulgar numbers. But it was accurate enough to say that notwithstanding my fortunate rent arrangements and the impression conveyed by my general unrestrained spending, I was close to ruin. A combination of factors was to blame. After years of hand-to-mouth commissions, I had hoped a regular role advising Nikolai would put me on a more dependable economic footing. In fact, the Russian's initial largesse almost immediately started to taper off, even as he made it clear he disapproved of me doing 'favours' for others – which I was nevertheless and with increasing desperation obliged to do, hence my involvement in Roland's pursuit of the luggage company.

My outgoings meanwhile were as numerous as ever. Often these took the form of professional disbursements. My duties to Nikolai and the need to find new business both involved being seen at the right places, which entailed membership fees, sartorial obligations and so on. On top of this my socialising – and almost every day there would be something: lunch at the Connaught or a box at Covent Garden or a liquid afternoon at Lord's – always ended with me picking up the bill. I did this out of good manners but fundamentally as an investment, since people mostly felt the need to repay a favour.

Just as frequently, however, my bank account was depleted by weakness and indiscipline; in that respect the impulsive acquisition of the Saint Laurent statuette was not unusual behaviour. I had reached a point where my supposed life of leisure was not only unaffordable but in some ways more draining than any regular office existence might have been. But that – a life of *normalcy*, the American word was suitably grotesque – was perhaps the only thing to which I was wholly and scrupulously opposed.

At the rooftop bar above Centre Court I ordered a flute of champagne before wandering over to the steel and glass railing. I watched the tennis fans milling around. Some of them would have queued overnight to have the chance of seeing the matches on the outer courts which the TV cameras never bothered with, and where in the absence of any formal seating one could get close enough to watch the sweat forming on the players' brows.

A Lebanese socialite and fixer called Nayla Duez was at one of the nearby tables. We were on friendly terms without exactly being friends; though she gave no sign of it I didn't doubt that she'd registered my presence. She was talking to a chap with a thuggish, foreman-turned-caudillo face. Probably Venezuelan, I decided: a *Chavista* who now the leader was gone was making his bid for respectability.

In the petrodollar hierarchy this man was lower than a Russian. If I strode across the terrace, making sure to catch Nayla's eye at the right moment, I would be signalling the sudden decline in my status and economic circumstances. From there, things would unfold in foreseeable fashion. I would flatter him with some brief discussion in Spanish about the natural beauty of his country, the immaculate coral reefs at Los Roques and paradisal private islands of La Tortuga and La Orchila. This would be followed by a cooler remark about Caracas, which he was not supposed to enjoy but would encourage his confidence in me. I'd show mild interest on learning he was thinking of investing in some property. Airily I'd mention that I knew some people in Switzerland and Guernsey and the British Virgin Islands – for maximum discretion and tax efficiency it was not at all unusual to end up with a property ownership structure incorporating all these places: a BVI company owned by a Guernsey company, both with Swiss bank accounts. (I wouldn't refer to my own far more modest experience in this field. Many years ago I used to act as legal owner of trusts holding American real estate for Mexican beneficiaries; it made tracing the money difficult, and I'd take a commission.)

Possibly the *Chavista* would confirm his interest in acquiring both tax residency and non-domicile status in this country – which may, with the right advice, and a Labuan bank account, have the effect of avoiding his fiscal liability anywhere in the world. How funny, I would reply, I happened to know a rather brilliant tax lawyer called Charlotte Turner, a Queen's Counsel no less. Not inexpensive. I'd buy a second bottle of champagne and take care to introduce him to suitable people: City grandees; with luck a minor member of the aristocracy, though not Antonia if I could help it. Perhaps Nayla (conceding defeat, but banking the favour) would mention my friendship with Nikolai. I'd have to make a phone call or two afterwards and probably invite him to dinner at the Imperial; but from this conversation I might hope ultimately to make back in kickbacks and finders' fees the tens of thousands I'd already spent on the Wimbledon debenture.

Except even before I had finished indulging this thought I registered the hungry manner in which the *Chavista* was looking at Nayla, and I knew he wasn't going to be interested in my contacts, however advantageous they were from a strictly rational perspective.

The holy grail was not retired Latin American generals or even Russian oligarchs. It was the Arabs – for their money, but also because if one struck lucky they were cultured men or at least anglophiles. They'd been to public school, they loved horse racing and muddy Land Rovers and probably owned a Gainsborough or two. By 6 p.m. their staff were in white ties. *Great Houses of London* could be found in their libraries. But of course Nayla Duez would have sooner clawed her eyes out than let me near someone like that.

I took a sip of champagne – it seemed bad luck to abandon it untouched – and returned to Onslow Square without speaking a word to anyone.

II

I had no idea where among the many millions of books within the British Library the section on medieval market crosses was to be found. Fortunately, Harold Highclere was a man of dependable habits and Antonia had mentioned a corner of the Rare Books Reading Room where he liked to work.

In some ways it was surprising that a man with his appreciation of history and architecture would choose to spend such a large proportion of his life here. Antonia thought it had something to do with having spent his formative years in the equally hideous library at Cambridge, whereas my own theory was that Harold saw something appealingly Protestant about making the journey each day from his Kensington home to the comparatively squalid King's Cross. And if from the exterior the national library resembled a cross between a vast Orwellian super-ministry and provincial leisure centre, he probably approved of the implied faith this showed in the larger metaphysical qualities of the books inside.

When I entered the mostly empty reading room, he seemed immersed in several arcane texts, but leapt to his feet as soon as he saw me. The rather frenzied response wasn't a surprise: I knew exchanging a word in here or even implying such an intention greatly offended his sense of propriety.

Occasionally I wondered if Harold would have made everyone happier if after university he'd joined a Trappist order. Some cosy monastery in Ghent, perhaps. We stood outside the room while he blinked and pinned his ancient-looking spectacles to the point between his eyebrows – he used the tip of his index finger, as if indicating for the bene-fit of a firing squad concealed somewhere nearby. As usual he wore faded cords and a checked Barbour shirt, and gave off a musty scent that seemed to affirm his dedication to the yellowing pages around him.

For all his eccentricities Harold was a gentleman. He was delighted, he said in a perfectly enunciated semi-whisper, that I had decided to visit him in this impromptu fashion. There was no trace of archness in his manner of speaking, which tended to fool stupid people into thinking he was not alert to the humour of things, including himself.

'Harold, I'm sorry to disturb you – I won't stay long.'

'Not at all. My wife will be very grateful; she thinks I spend far too much time with my books. She's right, of course. Shall we have a cup of tea?'

We went to the canteen on the first floor, in virtual dark-ness compared with the blazing sunshine outside. Harold insisted on paying, only to discover he might not have quite enough change for our two Earl Greys. Laboriously, he counted out the small mound of coins he'd produced on emptying his pockets, apologising repeatedly to the Portuguese girl behind the counter. (I was tempted to point towards the wall near the main entrance to the library, where his name was included in a list of benefactors.) When he found the right amount of change a look of immense satisfaction settled on his features.

'I gather you're reading about market crosses,' I said, after we'd sat down.

Harold shot a jealous glance at a more secluded corner table, lit just then by the glare of doctoral-student laptops.

'Oh yes, yes,' Harold said, 'that's right.' Despite his cherished scholastic privacy, I saw that he immediately accepted Antonia's decision to tell me the subject of his research. 'And how – how is everything with you?' he asked.

'Very well, thank you. Enjoying the weather.'

'Yes, I gather it's been hot – I haven't been outside much . . .'

'I suppose you're used to the heat.'

'Really?' He seemed rather fascinated. 'Why do you say that?'

'Well, because you grew up in Africa.'

'Oh yes, of course,' he said, frowning.

There was a further gentle stirring of his features: he perhaps thought he ought to make some sort of reciprocal enquiry, and then saw with relief I had no desire to discuss even meteorological aspects of my childhood. He took a sip of tea, and when he looked up again his smile was genuinely warm. 'And how is the – you know, the business thing?'

I suspected Harold was a more eloquent man than he let on, but couldn't bear the idea of appearing to flaunt his command of language. It partly accounted for his refusal ever to publish, as well as his reclusiveness more generally. 'Actually, it's been better,' I said, forcing myself to drink the tea. I was slightly envious of the quiet pleasure Harold was taking in his Earl Grey. It was cool in the library – I felt a chill rivulet of sweat work its way down to my hip – but I didn't by nature enjoy hot drinks when the temperature outside approached ninety degrees.

As expected, he was not interested in hearing the details of my hinted professional difficulties. Nor did his annual presence on the *Sunday Times* rich list leave him with any compulsion to make an awkward offer of a financial loan, or any other type of assistance. At that moment it occurred to me I might have liked Harold more than any other man alive.

'I was wondering,' he said, 'if you were going to the Cartier Foundation event?'

'As a matter of fact, I hadn't heard about it until I bumped into Ingy Vowles last Friday. What about you?'

'Oh, no! I shouldn't think so. I was, however, hoping you might be going. In fact, if you could be persuaded to do so I'd consider it something of a favour . . .'

'I'd be happy to,' I said with feigned indifference, 'if that would be useful.'

'My wife has so many friends. I confess I don't keep up with her life as much as I should, but I know how particularly fond she is of you. It's a great reassurance – to both of us – that she can rely on your good judgement.'

I was on the verge of replying with some banal phrase, when he went on, 'There are people of whom one ought to be wary. I think you know this better than me.' Harold had his hands flat on the table, a slightly childlike gesture. His fingernails were clean but a fraction long. 'If I call the Foundation myself it ought to secure your inclusion on the guest list. I know one or two of the directors, through my family,' he added, in typically oblique reference to his billion-pound diamond fortune. 'But perhaps that's already occurred to you.'

Clever little mole! Without any notion of the relevant facts or details, Harold had sniffed both the danger to his wife and my motive for calling on him so unexpectedly. If Antonia was bringing along Héctor Comala to the Cartier party I was determined to be there. For exactly what purpose, I hadn't yet decided – I only knew Nikolai had still not made any effort to contact me, and without the assurance of his protection the current situation was becoming unpleasantly tense. Merely coming home to the Onslow Square flat was something of an ordeal. I hadn't changed the front door lock, even though I knew Héctor must have the spare Yale set missing from the pockets of Diana's blood-soaked jeans. In the end what would it achieve – certainly not keep out the Mexican, if he resolved to pay me a visit – except show him I was afraid?

In thanking Harold I was careful not to make the sort of fuss that might embarrass him. Instead I quickly changed the subject, and asked after Antonia.

'She's at the tennis today – at least I believe so. If you'd like to join her, and if we can find a telephone, I could perhaps confirm this with Mrs Sharpe. Oh dear, I wonder if I have change for a call . . .'

'Thank you very much,' I said, rather chilled at the prospect of another episode involving small change, 'but this afternoon I'm intending to visit my neighbour, Mrs Belsey. She had a minor heart scare last week. I'm glad to say—'

'I don't think I know her.'

'No. Well,' I said, 'I should let you get back to your reading. Once again I hope you'll forgive the interruption.'

'Oh, not at all! Do surprise me like this on another occasion – I've rather enjoyed it.'

I considered myself warned. 'Well, goodbye, Harold.'

12

Mrs Belsey was in the hospital's private wing, where she had a room to herself. Our routine, clearly established by this visit, my third, was that I would arrive with tea and carrot cake from the nearby bakery. We'd remark on the run of hot weather. Then I'd read to her from a copy of the *Telegraph* I'd brought with me. (I'd have already checked to confirm it contained no item about Diana. Even if it had, I would naturally not have brought such an article to Judy Belsey's attention.) To try to minimise her appetite for any sort of news in my absence, I made sure to keep reading longer than she wanted or could possibly maintain her concentration for, until she would finally rally from her dozing to observe, with only the thinnest attempt to make a joke of it, that she really felt sufficiently informed of world events for one day.

Though a Wednesday, the atmosphere felt Sunday after-noonish – oddly deserted to one unused to the rhythms of the place. Mrs Belsey's eyes were closed when I arrived but she wasn't sleeping. On the plasma-screen television, which one of the nurses must have left on mute, a fortyish male reporter was talking in front of the NATO building in Brussels.

She seemed not to hear when I asked if she wouldn't prefer me to turn the TV off, making made me wonder if she already had no difficulty screening out trivial disturbances. The set itself was rather baffling for a person who hadn't owned one in decades: for one thing the immaculately sleek surface seemed to have been achieved at the expense of a power button. I spent a little time fussing – there was no sign of the remote control – but decided I couldn't do so indefinitely given the silent images were evidently not bothering Mrs Belsey. In the end I gave up and took my usual place in the more austere of the two visitors' chairs flanking the patient's bed.

'You shouldn't bring me this carrot cake. I haven't been so spoiled since I was a girl.'

'Actually, I've been sparing you – they also have berry and custard brioches.'

'Wicked!'

'Chocolate pecan brownies . . .' I said, though the humorous moment had passed.

One side of Mrs Belsey's face was slightly collapsed, a by-product of the old stroke. Before the heart attack this had been only subtly discernible. But now her former gaunt alertness was replaced by a sagging of the flesh, and it was this faint suggestion of fogginess and panic which – for all her concerted nonchalance in conversation – drew one's gaze to the thin black slant of her mouth.

Another effect of the heart attack was that the previously faint slur in my landlady's voice now came through more strongly: more than ever one was left with the cruel impression that she, who was so proudly abstinent, had been drinking on the sly.

I'd unfolded the *Telegraph* and was drawing breath to read the piece on the front page least likely to interest a convalescing octogenarian, when seemingly out of nowhere I heard Mrs Belsey exclaim: 'My goodness!' She scrabbled to sit up straighter in bed. 'How kind of you to drop by.'

I felt a familiar mild apprehension as I stood up to greet the visitor. Saying the wrong thing, or even not quite the right thing, was liable to disappoint Antonia. Not that she would have made it known in any obvious way, in the manner of Ingy or Camilla. Rather, one felt the beneficiary of an elegant understanding which stopped just short of forgiveness.

And to be in Antonia's disfavour, perhaps because it was always subtly expressed, and apparently without malice, could have broader impoverishing effects on one's social life.

'Oh, you're busy,' she said smoothly. 'I'll come back.'

The words sounded sincere even if it was also evident Antonia didn't expect to act on them. She didn't greet me. I couldn't tell if this was her shy dignified way of recognising an intimacy between us. A further thought occurred: that she knew – perhaps from speaking to Ingy and Harold, or simple intuition – that I was making regular visits to Mrs Belsey, and this had something to do with her unexpected decision to drop by the hospital.

'No, do stay! We weren't going to discuss anything important.'

A little sheepishly Mrs Belsey added, 'William – do sit down, both of you – William has been good enough to visit me every day since he heard of the – of what happened.'

Antonia gave me a distracted glance before returning to the patient. 'How *are* you?'

'Mostly I'm embarrassed. I don't see how I can go in the bookshop again.'

'Nonsense!'

Mrs Belsey for once looked slightly chastened. There was even a hint of pleasure – as if she'd been waiting a long time for someone to be stern with her. 'I saw a photograph of you in the paper,' she said. 'You were in the crowd at Wimbledon with a film star. William tells me he's very famous.'

If there was nothing she wanted to say Antonia had no fear of silences. Certainly she never gossiped about her friends. But since Mrs Belsey was not really part of her world, and moreover unwell, she said graciously, 'When I met him he was like me, just a model. I persuaded a theatre director friend to let him audition for the role of Ariel in *The Tempest*. He had this wraithlike beauty – mischievous and sad. I never imagined he'd end up in Hollywood.'

'I should think that cheered him up a bit,' said Mrs Belsey sensibly.

'Not especially, I'm afraid.'

I remembered the actor tried to kill himself last year. There had been a big fuss about it in the papers, though it wasn't the sort of thing that would have registered with Mrs Belsey.

'Well. I always think the melancholic types are more interesting than the rest of us.'

I thought of her deceased husband John; a more even keel would have been hard to find.

'I'm sure you're right,' Antonia said. Her black onyx eyes settling on me she added, 'Though I wonder if they can also be more ruthless, because of their need to protect themselves.'

'Oh . . . No, *quite* . . .' My landlady too was now looking at me, only more imploringly.

What could I say? That I thought the visitor melancholic, and interesting, and if required herself delicately ruthless?

'Antonia, can I get you some tea? Mrs Belsey?'

'Judy,' said Mrs Belsey.

'Judy,' I said.

They both declined. When the conversation moved on to the day's events at the tennis, Mrs Belsey showed her relief by nodding indiscriminately at everything her visitor said. Even for one so securely upper middle class, the idea of a strained and ultimately failed encounter with a distant relative of the Queen would be almost as anxiety-inducing as the original heart attack. Especially since they were really no more than acquaintances, two longstanding English residents of Kensington, and Antonia had left a thrilling match on Centre Court to sit at the octogenarian's bedside.

Her lopsided smile hadn't wavered but Mrs Belsey's eyelids were beginning to grow heavy. Quite apart from the drugs she was on and the shock her system had suffered, thanks to me she had been forced to do a lot of listening lately, and this did not come very naturally to her. I remember the tennis would be showing on the BBC, which might ease the strain of any looming pauses in the conversation. From my bedside seat I craned my head to look at the television.

I once met a psychiatrist at the Carlton Club ('savannah for a game hunter!') who, despite making a good living medicating fund managers, cited approvingly William James's belief that civilisation was best understood as a decline in proper occasions for fear. The sight which greeted me on the TV screen was unmistakably anxiogenic. A different journalist, this time a young woman in a head-scarf, was standing in front of a Georgian townhouse in Mayfair. I recognised it immediately as the Mexican embassy. The headline filling the lower half of the screen read MISSING MEXICAN SCHOOLGIRL: POLICE 'EXPECT WORST'.

Antonia was gamely describing the atmosphere on Centre Court with the new movable roof in use. She was too discreet to make any mention of my change of colour, though I was certain I saw her glance round to see what had caught my attention.

I felt a sickening alertness. In one way, the unfolding media story was nothing unexpected. But as time had passed since the night of the Tate party – twenty-four hours, then several days, then a week – with still no mention of Diana in the papers, I'd increasingly indulged the idea that her disappearance would go more or less unnoticed by the world.

This perhaps wasn't entirely delusional on my part: with her father in Mexico likewise 'disappeared' (as far as I knew) and her mother already dead, she had no immediate family to hold tearful press conferences. Then there was the blunt fact of her nationality. Unlike in the United States, in England people from Mexico weren't thought of as a serv-ant class of valets and cleaners, or worse illegal wetbacks, but only because mostly they weren't thought of at all. The

British were a pragmatic island people, and Mexico was a distant place which didn't threaten their sovereignty like continental Europe or their security like Russia or Syria, or present their bankers and lawyers and accountants with lucrative opportunities like the rising Asian economies. There was no shared language or colonial history between the two countries.

'It's rather stuffy,' I said, hearing the nervous false cheer in my voice. 'As if one's trapped in an enormous greenhouse.' With a growing sense of panic I realised Antonia had made an identical remark moments earlier. From the way her eyes opened and proceeded to settle bulgingly on me, even the drugged and infirm Mrs Belsey sensed some strange shift in my mood.

Perhaps the school, discovering that they couldn't get hold of Rafael, had asked the police to delay any public statement on their missing student. Or perhaps it had taken a few days for the media to notice Diana's telegenic looks. Even the Lope de Vega school might on a little digging turn out to hold some interest. The place had recently established a fee-paying British section as a way for the cash-strapped Madrid government to subsidise Spanish places, which meant that as well as the scions of Latin diplomats and even the odd minor Spanish royal – no doubt the reason Rafael had sent his daughter there – its pupils included the colourfully troubled offspring of well-heeled natives. Why else would these local children not be at more traditional London schools?

'I wonder,' announced Mrs Belsey drowsily, 'if this match is showing on the television. I hate the idea Antonia might be missing it on my account.'

I said nothing. I *did* nothing, except wait for my landlady to glance up at Diana's face on the screen to say, in a puzzled voice, 'Oh, look William – they're talking about your goddaughter!' Even if Antonia were prepared to believe I had a Mexican goddaughter I'd never spoken of before, she would be alarmed to learn the same girl – whose mention on the news caused the colour to drain from my face – had been reported missing very soon after Mrs Belsey had seen her visit my flat.

I was conscious that I had never learned what Héctor had told Antonia about my past in Mexico. Could he have made some casual reference to Diana Domínguez Saavedra – even alluded to a connection between me and the girl, despite the fact I hadn't even known of her existence until recently?

Either way, I feared Antonia would feel bound to contact the police, with whom there were plenty of matters I had no wish to discuss. The apparently odd fact, for example, that in my sole meeting with Diana Domínguez Saavedra I'd given her the keys to my flat. Or that years ago I'd introduced the girl's father to a bloodthirsty drug cartel, whom it seemed he'd stolen from. In a similar vein, I wasn't impatient to explain to the UK authorities that I believed the cartel's former inside man in the Mexican equivalent of the FBI – who now enjoyed protected diplomatic status with the embassy in London – had followed Diana to Onslow Square, where he'd killed her as retribution for her thieving father, or to drive me mad, or out of pure sadistic pleasure; still less confess to some box-ticking bobby that the oligarch I advised had arranged for the disposing of the girl's body to avoid her murder sullying his name by association.

At the very least – if I cooperated with the Metropolitan Police, and perhaps came to an arrangement with the British intelligence services – my social career in London would be over. That meant financial ruin.

And if I declined to cut a deal, where would I go? Returning to the States would displease the DEA and by extension Langley. The War on Terror creation of a European arrest warrant meant anywhere in the EU was ruled out if I didn't want to be immediately surrendered back to the UK. Since the financial crisis, Switzerland was eager to show it was no longer a haven for white-collar criminals. Nor would Nikolai tolerate me fleeing to Russia – beyond the reach of Scotland Yard and Europol, but where I knew too much of interest to my patron's enemies, meaning that he may be persuaded to take certain precautions not hard to arrange in that lawless jurisdiction. That's if those same enemies didn't get there first.

The prospect of starting again at fifty-one – finding myself in a godforsaken corner of the Far East, or more likely South America – was more than merely unappealing. I wasn't sure I could do it.

Seconds passed and still Mrs Belsey didn't lift her gaze as far as the television behind me. I felt no relief. She might have been tired and foggy, but she was essentially of sound mind. Her eyesight remained as hawkish as ever. The longer I went without responding the more likely she would at last look upwards, or Antonia would turn round. For all I knew Héctor Comala was right now sharing the screen with an image of Diana, gravely expressing his government's concern for the vanished student.

'William?' said Mrs Belsey thickly. 'Are you all right?'

'Sorry. Yes—'

'I think you were looking for the remote control earlier.'

'Yes . . .' I said again, helplessly. In my side-vision I was aware of Antonia watching me with interest.

A nurse entered the room. She bustled mutely around, readjusting the angle of Mrs Belsey's bed and flipping through a Manila patient file. At one point she took a zapper from her pocket and pointed it at the wall. The silence was broken by the arrival of the consultant: a short South Asian lady whose irrepressible gaiety was familiar from my previous visits. She immediately and beamingly made it clear that it was time for Antonia and me to leave. I sprang to my feet, ignoring the collective surprise at my own almost hysterical cheer.

I knew the essentials of my situation remained unpromising. If the Diana story remained in the news Mrs Belsey would come across it sooner or later (unless she died, which it seemed she wasn't going to do imminently). I was fairly certain I was shortly going to run out of money. And Nikolai had probably already cut me adrift. *I'm in a jam, old boy.* But the euphoria of the moment had given me a new sense of purpose. The first thing was to insist on somehow speaking with Nikolai, however personally humiliating and whatever the Russian's reluctance.

As we stepped into the sunshine of the Fulham Road, Antonia said she gathered I was coming to the party at the Mexican ambassador's house the day after tomorrow. In my adrenalin-charged state I may have only imagined the note of strain in her casual remark, or the marshalled naturalness with which she studied me. Either way, the looming event was a reminder that, whatever the faint chances of resolving my other problems, the one I had most cause to fear was Héctor Comala.

Part III

13

It was all very well being famously elusive, but now there was someone I really wanted to track down I discovered I had little idea of how this was done.

Normally I tried to limit my visits to One Hyde Park – I found it vulgar, and Nikolai was impossible to fool – but I was an approved visitor and therefore permitted entry to the lobby. The concierge (English, ex-army) sternly announced that the Russian was not in residence. If I wanted to wait, however, I was welcome to use the facilities. Perhaps I felt like a swim or sauna, or a session on the golf simulator? In the meantime, there were fresh pastries, coffee, juice . . . He was loud and faintly mocking in the public school manner; only a slight flush on his cheeks hinted at the shame he must have been feeling.

It was understandable the residents should take pleasure in being fussed over by Sandhurst-trained Anglo-Saxons. As a statement of luxury it was far more imaginative than the gruesomely whimsical chandelier, for example, which might just as easily be found in Beijing or Delhi or Lagos.

'Thank you but I'm already late for another meeting,' I lied. 'Please make sure his personal staff tell him about my visit.'

The concierge smiled with blokeish menace. 'We'd do that anyway.'

I'd telephoned Nikolai's Mayfair offices before leaving Onslow Square – I hadn't felt like another face-to-face encounter with Maksim if it could be avoided. The receptionist told me Nikolai was not in the office, and then politely stonewalled my request to be put through to certain other men whose stakes in the company's underlying assets were a fraction of the oligarch's. Needless to say they were all very rich.

I decided to make an uninvited trip to Mallott Hall. It was an ignominious option, however I thought it possible that Nikolai, who bored easily, had already returned from Thailand or wherever he'd gone next. Furthermore, I doubted that anyone was lying in telling me he wasn't at the Mayfair office or his Knightsbridge habitation – for one thing he didn't usually spend much time at either of those places. If I were truly persona non grata, as opposed to occupying some nebulous purgatorial position, I'd have been denied entry even to the lobby of One Hyde Park.

At the train station I shared a platform bench with a North African woman in a black robe and gold chiffon hijab. Above us the Shard flashed like an upturned knife in the cloudless sky. As the train pulled in, I began wandering towards the quieter carriages at the front. I'd almost reached the far end of the platform when I caught a glimpse of a slightly dishevelled middle-aged man emerging from the public loo. I had an instant and powerful sense he was the same jowly chap in a cheap suit I'd seen several times – too many to be unsuspicious – in Kensington.

Boarding the train, I looked back and saw that, except for a solitary member of railway staff, the entire length of the platform was now deserted. I couldn't be sure if the jowly figure had got in a different carriage, or if he had moved to the adjacent platform.

The train inched its way through the suburbs. The seats around me were empty and I tensed a little every time the carriage door opened and someone passed through. I was regretting not accepting the concierge's offer to use the private pool: for the last few days I'd been swimming two or three times a day, to have something to do between Mrs Belsey visits but also for the calming effect of the endorphins.

Finally, with great English deference the hills and fields of the Home Counties came into view. The little station where I got off (it appeared I was the only person to do so) consisted of two narrow platforms bisecting a sea of yellow rape fields. There wasn't even a ticket machine, so the locals evidently had to make do with an old-fashioned permit-to-travel dispenser and pay for their journeys on arriving at their destination.

It wasn't long before I was perspiring into my linen suit. The winding country lanes weren't designed for pedestrians and it was fortunate there was little traffic. Twice I was obliged to launch myself into the hedge, feeling a blast of warm air as speeding metal passed inches from my body. I regularly glanced behind me to check if anyone was following on foot, and continued to do so even after it became clear no sane person would undertake such an unpleasant and risky walk.

After about twenty minutes I came to a sharp bend in the lane. Immediately preceding this, on the left, was an unmarked turning. A lost or confused motorist who took it might wonder if he was still on a public road (he was not). Either way he would soon find himself admiring the thousand-acre estate, without noticing the discreet bulletproof cameras which monitored his presence. If he carried on as far as the closed metal gates, something about the guards – their physical aspects but also, up close, a deadness behind their eyes – would probably discourage him from asking for directions, which since they didn't understand English would in any case have been no use.

'My name is William Hoffer. I am friend of Nikolai Nikolaevich,' I announced in pompously stiff Russian.

The three plainclothes guards were evidently sceptical someone arriving at Mallott Hall on foot could make such a claim and hope to avoid a beating. But because I'd addressed them in their own language, or they were simply bored and decided on a whim to indulge me, the least imposing of the trio eventually wandered back into the gateside lodge. He left the door open and I saw him pause before picking up the telephone and dialling an extension number. An agonising lapse of time followed. Eventually, the skinny guard replaced the phone and the electronic gates began grindingly to part. All the while his colleagues maintained an impervious scrutiny of the middle-distance, as if it were all the same to them if I turned out to be Nikolai's long-lost bastard brother.

King Charles I had gifted the original estate to one of his favoured earls, whose increasingly impoverished descendants managed to cling on to it for generations until Nikolai came along. Much of the land was still farmed. I took some credit for this, though the traditional ways weren't maintained for sentimental reasons as much as from recognition that the neighbours were hardly powerless serfs. They were stockbrokers and City solicitors. There was an active local history society run by retirees with Oxbridge history degrees; an NHS board member and an editor of a broadsheet newspaper lived in the nearest village. It was rarely necessary to labour a point with Nikolai. Like him I came from a different world, but had rather more experience of blending into the background. If anything I was more obsessively attuned to the local culture than a native adviser would have been – or that presumably had been the Russian's calculation.

I strolled past grazing sheep and English oaks, and further off a row of Kentish oast houses where the hops of the estate were or had once been fermented to produce local ale. The whole bucolic scene made it feel slightly implausible that in showing up unannounced I was submitting myself to an uncertain reception.

The road dipped to reveal Mallott Hall. With its sweeping drive and landscape garden, its mansard roof and chateau tower, it resembled a filmset fantasy of aristocratic grandeur. Sir Sydney Wadhurst had written an epic poem admired by Tennyson about the life cycle of a farmworker on the estate. I'd never bothered to inform Nikolai his home was immortalised in the English canon, though no doubt Harold Highclere knew whole verses by heart, just as I was sure – lest someone tried to force him to recite a few lines – that if asked he'd deny ever having heard of it. Nikolai was between wives, so I had no idea who to expect at the house if it turned out he wasn't there. Nor did I know who had ordered the guard to open the gates for me. In the event I barely made it past the head butler, who loathed me and saw me as a phony: despite his conservative vowels he was from a little town near Cairns in Queensland, and our kind often spotted each other.

'Yulia!' I said in surprise at the person who came next to greet me.

For her part she gave no indication that there was anything unusual in my showing up out of the blue, or for that matter finding herself playing hostess. I hoped I was mistaken and her presence at Mallott Hall did not suggest she had decided to make her move. She was an accomplished designer, but not at all Nikolai's type romantically. I didn't want her to embarrass herself.

'You seem to have arrived on foot, William.'

Had she been consulted on the question of my admission on the premises? More likely, I decided, someone simply despatched her to find out what I wanted. 'There weren't any taxis at the train station.'

'What train station?'

'I wish I could put it down to religion, that I'm going through a Franciscan phase.'

Yulia's laugh revealed the tiny chip in one of her front teeth. 'Well, since you're not let's have afternoon tea, like Lord and Lady.'

We were in the library. Nikolai had probably never so much as glanced at them but I'd painstakingly chosen the books around us. Not far from my fingertips was a black leather-bound edition of *The Old Man and the Sea*, which I'd picked up in a street market in Havana. On the first page an inscription exhorted school pupils to take care of the book for the next generation. Its presence on these shelves had been a rather silly private joke, and I was tempted to slip it into my jacket pocket when Yulia's back was turned.

'Shall we sit outside?' she continued. 'It's such a beautiful day.'

'That would be fine – by the rotunda perhaps.'

'Don't they call it the "Pantheon"?'

I raised a sardonic eyebrow. 'Yes, I think they do.'

We wandered towards the lake, and were halfway across the bridge when Yulia broke the silence by asking when I thought British painting stopped being interesting.

'I suppose some people are waiting for it to start.'

'But I'm serious – when?'

'Are you asking for a date?'

'Of course.'

'About 1870 then. Since the Pre-Raphaelites, anyway.'

We arrived at the little temple and sat inside, near the statue of Aphrodite.

'William, what have you done?' said Yulia with sudden urgency. 'The last time I saw you, it was all: exhibition! Tate! Triumph!' She splayed her fingers, as if to mimic flashing bulbs. 'And now . . .'

'And now?'

She had brought her cigarettes with her; the lower half of the packet was taken up with the words FUMER TUE. 'Now he has that faraway look when your name is mentioned.'

'You think it's unpromising.'

'I think that's a very English word for what it is,' she said, expelling a stream of smoke.

A young man was crossing the lawn in our direction. With the loaded tray he was carrying his arms looked alarmingly spindly inside a white cotton shirt. I spotted among other items a jug of lemonade, a tower of assorted cakes and an enormous teapot. By the time he reached us his forehead was glistening.

Yulia gave some command or other in a dialect I couldn't follow, a mix of Russian and Yiddish it seemed. The boy nodded shyly and poured the tea. He left without glancing at us.

'Is Mrs Pritchard still running a tight ship?' I said in a guarded voice. The housekeeper, who found the security contingent trying enough, never hired domestic staff from outside the Commonwealth.

'She has gone,' said Yulia, with a triumphant wave of her cigarette.

'Ah . . .'

'Mrs Pritchard decided I was a greedy peasant girl from Odessa. Ideas above my station.' Yulia smiled icily. 'She was right, of course.'

'We're all Odessan peasants, proverbially speaking.'

'I'm not so sure. Even for our proverbs I think you have too many real teeth. But you haven't answered my question.'

'Which was that?'

'Why they called the Israeli when you presented yourself at the gates. Why for that matter you presented yourself at the gates, like some orphan child . . .'

'The Israeli? Itai Aktsin is here?'

'Since yesterday.' She paused ladling clotted cream onto her scone – despite her rail-thin figure Yulia always had a huge appetite – and looked at me with a hint of fear. 'He's come because of *you*?'

Even if I were the confiding sort it wouldn't have been sensible to say too much to Yulia, who had her own priorities. 'The problem is not of my making as such. It followed me.'

'From where?'

I decided it was simplest to say 'the past' and leave it at that.

Yulia cupped her palm beneath a scone as she raised it to her mouth. 'It doesn't matter if it's not your fault.' A spot of cream was left on her upper lip, which she brushed off with her finger, and then smiled at my pretence of not noticing. 'To him, I mean.'

'Let's not talk about my tedious business. Tell me, how are you?' I made a mental note to excise *Tell me* from my speech, a Hispanic tic I'd probably unwittingly picked up from Agustina. My housekeeper was the only person I spoke to more or less daily and she began half her sentences with *Dígame, Señor Hoffer . . .*

'Anyway you'll be careful,' advised Yulia, who knew better than to persist with the subject, not least for her own well-being.

'How's the scone?' – rhymed with 'con' and 'gone'. The thought of the dry heavy cake made my stomach clench but I took one from the plate.

Yulia watched me detachedly. 'As for how I am – aren't I here now, at Mallott Hall?'

'I wish you luck.' I said it sincerely, though if she had any sense she'd already consigned me to history. At the very least my endorsement would no longer count for much.

113

A little shrug: 'I'm too old, too clever,' she said with former-Communist frankness. 'But I must try.'

'Of course. One must try.'

'When I think of all the handsome men . . . You should be proud of your appearance, William. Anyone can be beautiful at twenty-five or even thirty-five! At fifty it requires a certain art.'

'Orwell thought everyone had the face they deserved by my age.' I took a sip of cooling tea, smiled. 'You look sceptical, rightly I think. Incidentally, make sure the new house-keeper is English. And get rid of that boy before Nikolai returns. He' – by that I meant the oligarch – 'didn't do all this to be reminded of home.'

The Israeli lived in Moscow, from where he provided Nikolai with advice on security matters. In that sense he performed a similar role to the oligarch's Mayfair consult-ants, albeit the range of services he provided was rather different from a company with a glossy website and two former British defence ministers among its non-executive directors. (The silent thugs who removed Diana's body from my flat reported to Itai Aktsin, needless to say, and not the respectable people in Mayfair.)

The fact Itai was ex-Mossad would not in itself have inspired Yulia's look of fright. She wasn't especially squeamish, and besides the world was awash with former intelligence and Special Forces types who'd turned free-lance. Nor was he a physically imposing presence: more than anything, he reminded me of a reedy Swiss bank manager. I once mentioned to him – light-heartedly, though it was perfectly true – that in Japanese his first name was an acknowledgement of pain, roughly the equivalent of 'ouch'. He was a person who inspired such idiotic remarks. He looked at me curiously, and in that moment I had the impression he was calculating my threshold for inhuman and degrading treatment, the way an off-duty tailor might glance at a man and mentally take his measurements.

I wasn't surprised that Itai, who was not the hurried sort, might know of my presence at Mallott Hall without making any immediate effort to speak to me. Instead Peter Macdonald, the head gardener, intercepted me on the lawn and we spent an hour or so wandering the estate. We began by inspecting the watermill and Neptune in his grotto. In a Lancashire accent softened by years down south, he pointed to a section of elm trees that would need pruning, followed by the new green-painted wooden signs for a path that crossed estate land and which local walkers maintained was an ancient right of way. Despite thin evidence for this claim the previous owners had always diplomatically relented. Peter and I had formed an alliance in persuading Nikolai to follow suit, but Peter was becoming frustrated. 'It doesn't matter how many of these we make,' he said, nodding at the sober Mallott Hall estate notice affixed to a nearby stile, 'they won't keep their dogs on a lead. That means I can't let sheep graze in these fields. That means I've got to find someone to cut the grass, when we're busy enough as it is.'

'Yes, of course,' I said sympathetically. I was looking at a flat expanse at the foot of the hill. 'That's where the cricket ground used to be?'

Peter nodded. 'Have you had a chance to speak to him?'

115

I said I'd mentioned the subject but no decision had been taken. We started wandering back to the house.

'It's probably too late for this season,' Peter grumbled. Sensing he had crossed a professional line, he suggested rather obsequiously that I must have been an athlete in my younger days. A baseball man, was I?

'Well – a long time ago.'

'How does it compare?'

'Pitching and swinging are more natural movements than bowling and batting. I suppose that's one obvious difference.'

'You prefer it then – baseball?' He nervously stroked the ginger hairs on his forearm. Given his milky complexion the plan to retire to Andalusia struck me as perhaps unwise, not that I was entitled to judge those who made contingencies for their old age.

'I don't know I'd say that. I enjoy listening to Test cricket on the radio. Of course the matches can be dull in stretches, but then so can opera, so can lots of things.'

'The Indians are mad about the short game – it's all American-style razzmatazz and cheerleaders now. Got to change with the times,' he added, at once sanctimonious and, perhaps thinking of the current owner of Mallott Hall, slightly defensive.

'I'm sure you're right.'

The Lancastrian's face darkened. 'Looks like his lordship wants a word. I'll leave you to it.'

For a moment I thought he was referring to Nikolai. Then following his gaze I was just able to make out a slender figure in a rumpled jacket sitting out on the terrace. One of the man's legs was idly draped over the other. He seemed absorbed by the tranquillity of the English landscape garden; indeed, from his reposing outline one could easily imagine he'd made the journey from Moscow expressly for the privilege.

14

'I'm glad you're here.'

'You shouldn't be.'

'No, perhaps not. But I'd like to speak to Nikolai.'

The Israeli spoke slowly, with a more guttural voice than Yulia. 'No more Nikolai.' Beneath the silvery wisps at his hairline I noticed a liver spot or dangerously discoloured mole.

'I've been giving some thought to my career,' I said dryly. '"Professional development" I believe is the modern phrase.'

'Your great ambition – I have heard something of this.'

'Ah, yes?' I'd assumed my reputation, if I had one, was of a confirmed idler.

'To rebuild the cricket park.'

'I don't mean the cricket park – pitch!' I felt my face grow hot, as if I were fourteen years old again. 'I was thinking more of Venezuela. Perhaps I could become more directly involved in that sort of thing.'

Nikolai held a small amount of stock (the Kremlin was the major shareholder) in a defence company looking to sell weapons to the Venezuelan administration. The official government rationale for the purchase was the War on

Drugs, though the Colombians and others wondered why S-300 surface-to-air missiles were required to fight drug lords who not only had no fighter planes but were rumoured to include the government minister in charge of the very arms deal.

As might be expected, there were high politics involved. A few months ago Venezuela pleased Russia by voting against a UN resolution declaring Crimea's independence referendum invalid. The Americans were unimpressed. For that reason, like the Mexican shale initiative, I judged it a matter best steering clear of, but the fact was I had experience of acting as a go-between with Latin politicians and it was a skill that might now be put to good use.

I regretted not swallowing my pride and introducing myself to Nayla Duez's *Chavista* when I had the chance. My situation was desperate enough that, if helping with my Russian patron's more sensitive affairs might rescue my standing with him, I was prepared to risk upsetting the people at Langley. It also wouldn't hurt to show the Ortega cartel I had some connections. This was a relatively minor consideration, however – not because I was relaxed about Héctor Comala receiving orders from Matamoros to punish my imagined sins against the cartel, but because Igor Ortega had murdered his own brother knowing it would weaken the business and start a bloodbath. In other words there was no point acting as if this was a cool-headed strategist, amenable to reason and political calculation.

Itai was continuing his serene survey of the garden. He was not authorised to hold the sort of conversation I was pushing for, and was paying me the compliment of not spelling this out. It was rapidly becoming clear that the entire purpose of his four-thousand-mile round trip had been to deliver virtually the first words he'd spoken. *No more Nikolai.*

Though it turned out I was wrong. I'd already taken a few steps towards the library's French windows when I heard a familiar name.

Itai continued, 'He works at the embassy.'

'Yes.'

'What else do you know about him?'

What do *you* know? I wondered as I retook my seat, feeling the chair's intricate iron patterning once again press into my lower back. If it weren't for the present company I'd have already asked the Odessan boy to fetch a cushion. 'He's from Chiapas originally,' I said. 'Indian or mestizo – anyway poor. At some point he went north to Matamoros, presumably fleeing some local trouble he'd got himself into. The story is that Comala had a disagreement in a bar with Nicolas José Ortega's bodyguard. Igor, the younger Ortega brother, would have killed him for the inconvenience, but Nicolas José took him under his wing. It was a pragmatic decision; for one thing, he now had a vacancy for a bodyguard. Later he arranged for Comala to take a position with the Policía Judicial Federal. This was a special unit under the public prosecutor's office with the role of tackling organised crime. From there Comala moved to the state intelligence agency, then known as the DFS. Later he returned to the PJF, which was by now called the AFI, the Agencia Federal de Investigación. It's now disbanded, nothing to do with its extravagant record of corruption, merely that a new unit was sponsored by a more powerful cartel.'

'So. A narcocop.'

'He's resourceful. He advised the Ortegas on diversifying their business and worked out the money-flows. With the quantum involved this was obviously quite complex. It's also how his path would have crossed with Rafael Domínguez Saavedra – for years the Ortega brothers laundered funds through Rafael's construction business. Comala also ran a kidnapping enterprise in Mexico City, a sort of Ortega-AFI joint investment vehicle, with day-to-day operations subcontracted to a subsidiary gang.' When Héctor surfaced in London last year I'd called my contact in Mexico – the same one who confirmed the news of Rafael's disappearance – to find out what he had been up to since the end of the Reagan era. 'By all accounts it was very profitable,' I continued. 'Apparently he'd sometimes visit the kidnapped, whether a ransom had been paid or not. To amuse himself.'

Itai made an impatient swatting gesture. 'You've met this man?'

'When he was with the DFS it was understood he spoke not just for Nicolas José but the cartels more widely. They were more collegial back then. In any case, the agency wanted their own means of communicating with Héctor.'

'Separate to the local partners.'

'Precisely.'

'And this was you?'

I nodded.

'A special envoy to the cartels?'

'Nothing quite so grand.'

'You became friends? Something less?' he said. 'Something more?'

'I try to stay on good terms with people,' I said. 'It wasn't possible in this case. By the way, should I ask what happened – with Diana, I mean?'

In Mexico they used to throw a corpse in a hole and cover it in lime. *Leche*, they called it: milk. Nowadays they would probably leave a severed head on the windscreen of a patrol car.

'Who?'

'The body,' I said, 'the custom-made knife too, for that matter. I hate to sound ungrateful but Bob Kramer only makes a certain number every year. Demand is so high you can't simply *buy* them.'

'No.'

'I'm sorry?'

'The answer to your question.'

He was probably right. 'Nevertheless, I'm afraid the matter isn't quite finished.'

'You believe our friend has not helped you enough.'

'I'm not asking *him*.'

The Israeli's watery eyes narrowed as he scanned the lawn. 'This – all this – has come at a bad moment,' he said.

'The shale matter . . .'

'Does it really seem to you' – a wrinkle curved from the corner of Itai's eye into the hollow of his cheek; it took a moment before I realised he was smiling – 'we have no bigger worries than your spics?'

I grinned back at him, stung. He was referring of course to Russia and the prospect of a new Cold War.

'Like you, he prefers the life of the exile.' He stood up, made an indifferent effort to smooth his jacket. There would be a plane waiting. 'William Hoffer.' It was at once rebuke, statement of mild regret and nonchalant dismissal. 'A German name.'

I nodded.

'You speak the language?'

'A little.'

He recited the words with a certain relish: *he who fights with monsters should be careful lest he thereby become a monster*. 'Or something like this,' he added in English with a little shrug. 'Nietzsche.'

It was a hoary old line. But I remembered that the night I found Diana's body there was no sign of any struggle in my flat – no furniture upturned, no scratch marks on the door, no broken china – and I wondered if she'd looked into Héctor's eyes and straightaway seen there was nothing to be done.

I said, 'I admit I had more practical assistance in mind.'

Itai had moved from my line of sight. I waited but the retreating steps across the terrace didn't come. The skin above my ear tingled in readiness for – what?

'He's a nightwalker.'

'Nightwalker?' If this was code or a Yiddishism I had no idea of its meaning.

'Comala walks – in Green Park. At night. Between three and four in the morning.'

Hadn't a young man been found butchered in Green Park a few months ago? The details of the crime were sufficiently gruesome for the BBC radio bulletin to describe them in carefully imprecise terms, though I'd seen a lurid headline in the *Evening Standard*. I'd had no reason to pay particular attention to the incident, and barely glanced at the text of the article. But it *was* Green Park, I was sure of it, because for a few weeks afterwards a Member of Parliament had gone around calling for it to be closed after midnight like the other royal parks. I was deciding not to mention this when I saw Itai had already disappeared back inside the house.

15

The crocodile glistened from the hundreds of yellow diamonds embedded in its crescent form. The long jaw of its mate rested on its back, like a pair of lazing dogs. At the clasp the tails entwined. Something about their readied little legs – the sharp-clawed feet must have dug uncomfortably into the Mexican diva's breast – suggested the cosy arrangement was provisional; any moment the beasts might lunge.

I leant towards the glass case. The two pairs of eyes, marquise-shaped rubies and emeralds, completed the piece.

'Those were pearls, and all that,' said a loud male voice behind me.

'Roland – I didn't know you were going to be here.'

'At school I was frequently invited to copy out sections of *The Waste Land*. Come to think of it, wasn't T. S. Eliot another Kensington Midwesterner?'

He seemed in a good mood. Normally I wouldn't have considered this particularly auspicious, but on this occasion I hoped it meant a successful outcome with the luggage company acquisition. It might even turn out that my fee, or part of it at least, could be brought forward.

In these circumstances I had no interest in telling Roland the verse he'd half-quoted was originally from Shakespeare. Besides, it might well have been a double-bluff, and he was testing to see if the Ohio rube would dare correct him. (It seemed dimly coincidental that Antonia had mentioned *The Tempest* only a couple of days ago, but somehow of a piece with the dreamlike unfolding of the last fortnight.) 'As I recollect,' I said, 'Tom Eliot was from Minnesota.'

'Ah, Kent and Surrey situation, is it? Say no more. On a separate note you seemed to make the desired impression the other evening.'

'I'm glad to hear it.'

'With our confused young artist, I mean,' Roland added needlessly. He seemed vaguely irritated, perhaps having sensed he'd made a slight fool of himself a few moments ago. For Roland there was no shame in philistinism as long as one drolly owned up to it; to do so unwittingly was another matter. 'Your powers,' he said, 'whatever they are exactly, are as sharp as ever.'

'You mean he's agreed to sell to you?'

'Not yet. But the signs are good.'

'Well, if there's anything further I can do . . .' I made myself say.

'Excellent – just what I was hoping. He's over there, ogling the photos. I don't know if "ogling" is exactly the word.'

'Who is?'

Roland was beaming. 'The boy. Dorian. I thought he'd enjoy more or less every aspect of this evening: the film diva pictures, the hideous champagne margaritas, the even more hideous necklaces. You.'

128

There was enough to worry about this evening – notably Antonia and Héctor, neither of whom I'd yet spotted – without having to chaperone Roland's corporate prey. Sure enough, on the other side of the room I saw Dorian standing with hand in pocket, his waist-high flute held at a casual angle that risked spilling its contents on the ambassador's Persian carpet. His unruly black hair was tonight gelled into a neat side-parting and he looked worryingly unsteady. Though perhaps this wasn't the result of alcohol as much as his bad knee, which couldn't be trusted to support even his slender frame.

The photographic portrait he was admiring was part of a series loaned by the María Félix estate for the evening. It featured the actress looking windswept on a boat. In contrast with the opulently kitsch jewellery on display, the figure in the framed picture wore a simple cream turtleneck and little make-up. It ought to have looked absurd: the voluptuous *máxima diva* trying to pass herself off as wholesomely Nordic. Only somehow – possibly it was the sly smile suggesting the whole thing was just her way of driving Ingrid Bergman mad – the image was a triumph.

Roland said, 'Oh God. Here comes the Spanish disquisition.'

The ambassador was an arresting sight: a great bald bear dressed by an Italian. He was also famously verbose. He began by welcoming his guests to Belgrave Square, a good number of whom appeared surprised to learn they were here to celebrate 'The Year of Mexico in the UK'. (Certainly Ingy, when she first mentioned this evening, had made no reference to the cultural and commercial initiative jointly organised by the two governments.) He then thanked the

Cartier and Félix Foundations for making the evening possible. Having invoked the genius of the maison Cartier and in particular Jacques, the anglophile *frère* who created no fewer than twenty-seven tiaras for the coronation of Edward VII, the ambassador moved on to the equally prodigious *maestría* of María Félix, Mexico's supreme icon of the silver screen.

His sentences began to lengthen as he started to hit his rather notorious stride. Like María Félix herself, the beauty of the reptile pieces in the room this evening, and above all of the crowning masterwork – the special order for the film star, with its more than two thousand white diamonds, flecked with red and green scales (the national colours, of course, of Mexico) – was transcendent. But also like the actress, they had a special *mexicanidad*. The serpent was after all acknowledged in the national coat of arms and the flag of the Republic. Well, he continued, immediately countering himself again (in his life as a public intellectual he'd been known for his rather confusing Socratic monologues), in another sense that image – the eagle and the snake – was universal. Who did not know of the Aesop fable? Not to mention, talking of the snake as emblem of evil, the Garden of Eden. But in Mexico, where layers of identity and history were manifold, the story had roots in pre-Colombian mythology. Taking first the Aztec god, the feathered serpent Quetzalcoatl, where we find this idea of completion, bird and snake conjoined in their eternal struggle, beyond good and evil one might say, the very same image also referred to by Pliny the Elder in his *Natural History*—

'William, you made it,' said Ingy Vowles, in not quite a whisper and ignoring the glances of disapproval. Her face

130

this evening was painted white as the pox-ravaged Virgin Queen herself.

'I hope you're not too disappointed.'

'Much worse. I'm impressed. I felt I'd set you a little challenge when I mentioned it the other day, and now I *know* there's no gathering in London that's safe from you,' she said. 'How did you manage it, out of interest?'

'Actually it was Harold Highclere.' It was something of a challenge to say this discreetly enough not to irritate those listening to the ambassador's speech, but without alerting Ingy to the mischievous pleasure of speaking even louder herself.

'. . . Then of course Mr Martín Luis Guzmán, in his seminal work *El águila y la serpiente*, used this same image to explore the Revolution of 1910 to 1920—'

'Harold? Is he here?'

I shook my head. 'No, I don't think so.'

'Well, I've never *heard* of Harold doing a favour like that for anyone . . .'

There was an interruption from the back of the room. My first thought was a measure of relief that Ingy's bad manners would now be forgotten. Someone – I couldn't get a clear view of him – was shouting huskily, provoking apprehensive looks among the Mexican guests.

The closer the man got to the ambassador, who had by now fallen silent, the louder his voice grew. He must have been anxious to say his piece before the guards and embassy officials caught up with him. There was a chance he was making for the ambassador for a different reason, unlikely on the face of it, but then under the Vienna Convention we were effectively on Mexican soil and even Ingy must have

131

had an idea this was rather more blood-drenched than the rest of Belgravia.

Despite his anger the man sounded educated, so that I thought at first he might be a lawyer of some description. When I finally saw him, however, I realised he was more likely a university professor or investigative journalist. Lank hair spilled over his creased paisley collar, and his unshaven equine face (he was tall, over six foot) glinted with silvery stubble. As he barged past Roland there was a strong waft of stale tobacco. He was talking about a recent massacre carried out by the Mexican army. From the reports I'd read the victims were suspected cartel members, though I didn't hear him mention this.

In his country, the protester growled in Spanish, there was no legal definition of *masacre*, no basis in the constitution or procedural codes for prosecuting complicit state agents, no jurisdiction for civilian courts to try members of the armed forces. Waving his finger aloft like a priest, there was, he said, no special division of the Attorney General's office devoted to prosecuting state-sponsored killings.

Héctor Comala was not quite as tall as the other man, and hadn't yet spoken. But when the fight went out of the heckler no one seemed surprised, even those who had no idea who this man was who'd suavely stepped into his path. The entire room was mesmerised by the Tzeltal cheekbones, hallmark double-breasted suit and eerie smile. For his part the protester was looking suddenly rather timid and pale.

'My dear sir.' Héctor's silky voice was neither loud nor soft; neither mocking nor entirely earnest. 'Before you mentioned this abominable crime we were hearing of the plumed serpent. The Revolution which left a million dead.

132

I make no claim to His Excellency's oratory, but it seems to me one could say things about the practices of the past the essence of which might be that violence is not an unfortunate aspect of the Mexican condition; it is the condition.'

There was some uneasy tittering among the crowd. I glanced at the ambassador, who was smiling in slightly sickly fashion.

'Hell is empty, sir, and all the devils are in Mexico.'

At least someone knew his Shakespeare, I thought.

'Nevertheless, I can assure you a division of the Attorney General's office has been established. And the legal definition you speak of can be found in a report of the Chamber of Deputies published only last month.'

'I suppose you would know this. Of all people.' There was a faint quiver in the man's voice.

'Certainly I would.' Héctor smiled, revealing to the room the elegant disfigurement at his lip. 'I drafted it.'

'Clever old Antonia,' said Ingy, the drollness she was aiming for overwhelmed by her envy and excitement.

His hand at the other man's back, as if they were old friends off to have a catch-up, Héctor had loudly vowed to track down a copy of the Congress report. If necessary, he would personally escort the protester to the embassy library on St George Street.

Comala's intervention had rescued the party but taken the wind out of the poor ambassador's sails, having undercut His Excellency's central aim, at least to the extent his speeches could be said to possess such things, of reminding the distinguished guests that beneath the endless media stories of drug trade bloodshed – hundreds of thousands of dead and disappeared in the last few years, numbers that put Iraq or Libya in the shade – another Mexico existed of glamorous movie stars and exotic Aztec myths. Then the ambassador himself had raised an unhelpful ghost, with a concluding reference to the still-missing teenager; a student of exceptional intellectual talents who he had no doubt was in everyone's thoughts and prayers. As the ambassador spoke these words I sensed a discomforting rise of emotion in the room. It was a reminder that Mexico – home of the Day of the Dead, not to mention the sinister cult of Santa Muerte – was a country that fetishised death as much as beauty.

Diana might yet become a symbol of her country's suffering. It was even possible her cosmopolitanism could perversely encourage such an outcome. To my dismay, I'd already seen that *El País* and the *International New York Times* had covered the news of the teenager's mysterious disappearance, albeit without any great attention – only a single news-in-brief paragraph in both cases. But it was almost inconceivable that the Mexican media, flattered by the foreign interest in one of their citizens, wouldn't have also picked up on the story by now.

'I expect he's having a few of his chaps sort out that intolerably worthy old hippy,' Roland said. 'It's only a shame they won't do the same to the ambassador – I've met toddlers with more clarity of thought. Though I don't see what Antonia Highclere has to do with anything.'

Ingy leaned enigmatically. In the process she brushed against Roland's arm, who frowned as though disturbed by an irritating cat.

She said, 'I rather think if anyone knows the answer to that, it's William.'

'There's no point asking William to divulge anything. If you want *my* opinion,' said Roland, 'the Mexicans shouldn't do themselves down. Their methods seem quite admirable in many ways.'

'I'll just say hello to your guest.'

'Oh, yes, fine,' said Roland, as if he couldn't quite remember who I was talking about. He disliked even the most indirect mention of money in front of a woman – or rather of *his* money, or prospects of acquiring more of it. What made this attitude particularly puzzling was that he was married to an eminent tax lawyer who could scarcely have been less squeamish about the subject.

Making my way through the crowd, I saw that Antonia had arrived and was talking to Julian Vowles. She looked elegant as ever in a black velvet dress; hanging from her neck appeared to be a smaller and more tasteful Cartier serpent necklace than the one in the glass case presently being admired by Dorian.

'Oh, hey,' said the young man tipsily. 'I wondered if you were going to be here.'

I thought of him witnessing me smoke heroin in east London, and the regrettable rumours about my past he'd heard from his friend. 'What do you make of it?' I asked. His salt-rimmed flute, I noticed, was almost empty.

'It's the most diva-queen, fuck-you piece of jewellery I've ever seen. And I've spent, like, a *lot* of time in Los Angeles.' He took a swig of his champagne margarita. 'Who was María Félix, anyway?'

'A famous actress, at least in her time.'

'We're not talking about *telenovelas*. Otherwise I'd definitely know her.'

'No.'

'At school everyone was like, How come you're so good at Spanish when you suck at everything else?'

'She worked with Buñuel, Renoir, people like that.'

He nodded enthusiastically in a way that suggested he had nothing to add on this subject. In slight desperation I asked what he thought of his cocktail.

'Roland says anyone who puts lime juice in Bollinger should be horsewhipped.' He gave a quick guilty smile. 'I guess I've been knocking it back pretty fast. To be honest, I'm sort of nervous.'

'Well, it's quite an intimidating crowd.'

He looked confused for a moment. 'No, it's not about – I don't care about these people. Roland said you'd be here, but I didn't know if you'd be pleased to see me. It was a weird night a couple of weeks back and you're pretty hard to read. Probably you've been told that.' His cheeks had turned a dark cherry colour.

I could have easily said something to reassure or perhaps even thrill him. Instead I asked after the family business, ignoring the pout Dorian now directed at his red loafers. The flamboyance of the shoes was partly balanced by dark jeans and a black silk shirt. Along with his blazer – navy-and-mauve stripes with a vivid scarlet collar, from the recent E. Tautz collection – they suggested he wasn't completely without a sense of style.

'I don't know . . . It's not that I hate the company, or have some huge objection to capitalism.'

'You're an artist,' I said. 'This should be the focus of your energies, not running a struggling enterprise.'

'Sure! Exactly!' Dorian was nodding and sipping. 'The problem is I feel . . . not guilty exactly . . . But the fact is I disappointed my father – like, a lot – while he was alive. So now . . .'

From his beseeching expression I had the sense he wanted me to acknowledge something.

'Perhaps,' I began carefully, 'you feel a particular responsibility to uphold the family tradition. Being only half-English.'

He nodded gratefully. 'It's weird how you seem to understand me. Maybe it's because neither of us is completely one thing or the other. But whatever, it's nice,' he added coyly.

Before I could answer he went on, 'The funny thing is that, even though he's a vulture, my dad would probably have liked Roland Turner.'

'I don't really think that's a fair descript—'

'It's okay! You can relax,' Dorian said. 'I'm going to sign on the dotted line. Of course I could get more from the Russian guys . . .'

Ignoring his teasing smile – he knew I was wondering why he'd chosen the lower offer – I told him he'd made a wise decision, that Roland and his capital partners had a lot of experience at re-launching heritage companies.

'When were you thinking of formally accepting?' I asked casually. 'If you need a good lawyer – to represent you personally, I mean, not the company – I'm sure I can find someone who owes me a favour. You wouldn't have to pay anything,' I added, since I wasn't quite sure if he'd understood.

From his empty expression I saw that, despite dimly sensing its practical benefit, Dorian couldn't bring himself to take an interest in legal advice, free or otherwise. Hailing a waiter passing nearby with a drinks tray, he polished off the champagne margarita and swapped his empty flute for a full one. 'So I was wondering,' he said hesitantly, 'if you'd like to see my collage work sometime – since you're interested in art and everything. Roland says you know all the major dealers in London. Not that I want to *use* you,' he added with rather shaming sincerity. 'What I mean is, I'd love to show you my art and maybe hang out with you a little. No agenda.'

'I'd love to see your work. Thank you for the invitation.'

'Great!' He took out his iPhone. 'So I'll drop you a text?'

'I'm afraid I don't have a mobile telephone – or email.'

Dorian swore in histrionic disbelief just as the head of the British Council squeezed past. She frowned and gave me a rather wintry *Hello, William.*

'What about your landline, then?' the boy said. 'Or maybe you could give me your address in Kensington? We could *correspond*,' he said with mock gravity.

'It's true, we could. But I think it would be easiest simply to arrange a time now. I remember where you live in Little Venice, if that's where you keep your work.'

I saw the same injured-foal look from our last encounter, after I'd mistakenly repeated his friend's snide phrase. He wanted my contact information, I understood that; but in agreeing to see his art I was already meeting his implied condition for the sale of the business, and I couldn't be blamed if the young man wasn't driving a very hard bargain. Besides, I had other worries just now. Not unrelatedly, recent events didn't suggest it was sensible to encourage young people to think they could show up at my flat unannounced.

As if on cue Héctor reappeared, looking pleased with himself or rather with the effect he was producing on the English guests. Several of these hovered a few paces away, in the hope of catching his eye or securing an introduction from a useful Mexican. The amusing thing – at least it would have been, had it been anyone else – was that nothing prevented one of these loiterers from simply going up and talking to him, since he was standing by himself, absently cradling a glass of mescal in his palm. Of all those I'd observed in society over the years – presidents and prime ministers, artists and film stars – none matched Héctor Comala's native self-possession. Absurd as it sounded, he was like some serene god who saw the suffering men were capable of and considered it a moral or aesthetic duty to reveal this to them. And of course he was greedy.

'We can do that,' Dorian said a shade sulkily. 'I'm pretty much free whenever. So.'

'You don't spend much time at your company's head office then?' Along with everyone else in the room I was pretending not to watch Antonia glide towards Héctor. 'Duke Street, isn't it?'

'I don't go in *every day*. Only if there's some special meeting.' Dorian turned to follow my gaze. 'You know, in my old school dorm we used to have a picture of her on the wall. Someone put it up to annoy the house captain – or maybe suck up to him, I could never figure out which – because he was supposed to be a distant cousin of hers or something. She actually looks better in the flesh.'

'Do you mean Ant—'

'She's coming over now. With the guy with the lip-scar.'

For obvious reasons I didn't want Dorian meeting Héctor. 'We'll speak later to arrange the art visit,' I said curtly.

'Oh! Okay. But I might not stay much longer.'

'Then you can contact me through Roland.'

The young man's eyes were glistening. 'Well, I'll leave you to—'

'Yes, goodbye.'

They weren't far away now. A Mexican actor – in London to perform in a Lorca play at the Almeida, but who'd recently played a villain in a Hollywood film – called to Antonia as she passed by. She seemed not to hear but the actor reached out and clutched her arm. I watched her introduce Héctor, who said something to the actor in Spanish, slightly rudely, since Antonia didn't speak the language, though she gazed at him admiringly, as if in his brilliance he'd conjured this alien grammar and vocabulary out of nowhere. Certainly there was something other-worldly in the cold mid-sentence moment when I caught his eye, or rather when he chose to acknowledge the abandonment of my self-discipline as I stood staring at him. The next thing I was fleeing the room.

16

To reach Pall Mall it was simplest to cut through Green Park. Unsurprisingly – given the lateish hour and soupy air, which suggested the last fortnight's heatwave was about to break – the park was all but empty. A solitary group of Italian teenagers defied the imminent downpour. They sat in a circle, smoking marijuana and passing round bottles of cheap spirits.

It was perfectly possible Héctor Comala lived near the park, which was within walking distance of the Mexican embassy; but even if the Israeli's 'nightwalker' claim was true Héctor might not follow his usual routine after attending tonight's party, not least with a thunderstorm on the way. That assumed nocturnal strolls were his usual routine and not just something he did on odd occasions when he was unable to sleep.

I could have pushed Itai for more detail. Except he'd tossed me this scrap of information in the manner of a valedictory favour; something he wished himself and certainly Nikolai to have no involvement with, and I wasn't going to beg.

'Busy tonight!'

The man in black tie who said this was the only other occupant of the smoking room. He must have entered while my thoughts were drifting. I was sitting in a corner armchair, the same spot where Churchill had liked to doze after a long lunch, or so I'd been told. A book plucked more or less randomly from the shelves (Eachard's *The Grounds and Occasions of the Contempt of the Clergy and Religion Enquired Into*) lay abandoned in my lap.

It took me a moment to realise he was a law lord. The Right Honourable the Lord what of what? My memory, normally reliable with names, now drew a blank.

'Yes, indeed,' I said, only realising as I spoke the words that he was referring to the noise of a dozen conversations coming from the front hall, a sea of tinkling laughs and grave masculine pronouncements through which a great rumble now rose up. I thought for a moment of Roland and the thunder section of *The Waste Land*, but my mind, as if reluctant to expend energy on another subject, turned reflexively back to Héctor. I pictured him waiting for me outside in the storm, with Green Park in my rather fevered imagination a dark, Rousseau-ish jungle.

'Dickens Society dinner,' the judge said, drily acknowledging our sudden kinship, like scholars hearing a distant roar from the sports field.

A member of staff came in and apologised for the commotion. He addressed us both but stood closer to the law lord, who took in the special pleading – magnificent speech from a former prime minister, profusion of port – with a benign distracted expression. The staff member must have realised he'd gone on too long because he abruptly gave up on his chatter and asked us if we'd like a drink. The law lord declined with a thoughtless courtesy I knew I'd never quite pull off.

'I'll have a whiskey sour, please,' I said.

'Any particular bourbon?'

'Black Maple Hill if you have it. Thank you. I'm American,' I explained to the judge when the two of us were alone again.

'I might have heard something along those lines. Didn't pick it up from the accent.'

The slight mischief with which he said this produced no awkwardness. One sensed he wasn't a malicious man, and anyway his pronunciation was unimpeachable enough for both of us. He was also something of an endangered species. The title of law lord had been formally abolished a few years ago – a senior judge who also belonged to the legislature was thought to offend modern constitutional etiquette – though, under a somewhat convoluted compromise, existing office holders remained members of the House of Lords, except they were barred from sitting or voting there until their retirement from the bench.

When he closed his copy of *The Times* I knew it would have been rude to return to my book, not least as I so obviously wasn't reading it. The silence stretched; he was it seemed resolved to converse without having anything in particular to say.

'Had a pleasant evening?' I eventually offered.

'More or less, thank you for asking. I was at Covent Garden.'

'For the *Quixote*?'

He looked surprised for a moment. 'Yes, as a matter of fact. Do you know it?'

'I saw it at the Teatro Colón, a long time ago.'

'Ah, Buenos Aires . . .' he said, with a private enthusiasm that made me warm to him.

'How was this evening's performance?'

'I'm afraid I spent most of it composing the end of a judgment. In that sense it was rather wasted on me.'

'If it makes you feel better,' I said, 'you probably weren't the only one whose mind wandered a little.'

'Oh? What do you suppose everyone else was thinking about?'

I sensed his intrigue at the prospect of some new insight into human fallibility. Outside, meanwhile, the thunder-claps were getting closer. I said I couldn't speculate.

'Well, what sort of things do *you* find yourself reflecting on? During the longueurs, I mean.'

'I'm not sure I'm typical of most opera-goers, or any group for that matter. I hope that doesn't sound conceited.'

He gave me an appraising look. 'I gather you're a bachelor.'

'Yes.'

'Got a dog?'

'No dog.'

'Not a dog man?'

'I think I could be,' I said, after reflecting for a moment. 'The trouble is I live in a fairly small flat and I'm not there very often. It wouldn't be fair on my housekeeper.'

The staff member returned with my whiskey sour. He glanced at the law lord: it clearly occurred to him to check if the judge had changed his mind about a drink, but in the end he opted to slide bashfully away.

'You don't get lonely then,' he said, more summary than question.

'To be honest, if anything I feel I see too much of people.'

He smiled. 'It's funny.'

'What is?'

'You're not exactly how I expected.'

I sipped my bourbon. It wasn't the kind I'd asked for.

'Now,' he said with a sigh, 'I suppose I ought to finish writing this damn judgment.'

The rain was coming in great horizontal lines down the sash windows. 'You're off home?'

'Home? No, no. I'll be here tonight.'

'I see.'

He saw I didn't. 'We have a little place in Fulham. For the week, that is – home is Gloucestershire. But my wife prefers me to stay here on evenings like these.'

I was certain he was sober. Perhaps he meant she had some obscure objection to him travelling during a thunderstorm? It seemed unlikely.

'She can't stand having me pacing around, turning over phrases and so on. I often think the poor woman would've been happier marrying some brainless farmer.' He began to rise from his armchair and then stopped halfway. The sleeves of his dinner jacket trembled faintly from the weight of him. 'You're not related to any farmers?'

'Actually I come from a long line of them.' This wasn't an admission I'd made before, certainly not in London let alone the Imperial Club.

'In that case I'm sorry for my silly joke. No shame in the rural life.'

'They'd have certainly agreed with you.'

There was a great roll of thunder and a second or two later the windows flashed white. The law lord peered at the storm with vague distaste. He turned his back to me and, already walking away, half-raised a hand to signal farewell. The impoliteness of it was perversely pleasing, though of course I didn't imagine he considered us equals.

'Why not look into the dog thing,' he called over his shoulder. 'You might find your housekeeper rather enjoys the company.'

By 11 p.m. the downpour had stopped as abruptly as it had begun and I was turning from Haymarket onto Piccadilly Circus. I carried a long-handled umbrella the Imperial Club doorman had insisted on lending me.

The famous lights looked smudged, as if the scene were a watercolour by one of the street artists who since the storm had abandoned their posts. On the steps of Eros a pair of tramps with ruined faces laughed about something.

Ducking into the Criterion was less from prudent time management – I still had hours to kill before Héctor's supposed night-walk – than a general sense of apprehension on nearing Green Park. In short, I needed a drink. I realised I'd made a mistake before even getting through the swivel door. It was boorish to object to tourists, just as it was obvious that what filled me with alarm and repulsion – regardless of the complicit twinkle in the French bartender's eye – was not really the prescient Pac A Macs and non-alcoholic cocktails and general cheery disregard of the neo-byzantine ceiling. It was *me*, or at least the uncomfortable reminder of a past life – in the same way that, despite not being completely immune to Dorian's

American exuberance, his apparently boundless puppyish faith in me, there were times when I felt a wave of disgust that took me by surprise and afterwards filled me with guilt.

I sat at the bar and ordered a dry Martini. 'You don't have a cigarette, do you?'

The bartender surveyed me with interest. He was late twenties and spoke confident English; perhaps he had one of those degrees in hospitality his countrymen had developed an unlikely obsession with. I felt a slight pang for the days when French presidents would sooner cut their tongues out than utter a word of Anglo-Saxon and even the Republic's street sweepers had studied a little Montaigne. 'I can give you a cigarette,' he said. 'But you won't be able to smoke it here.'

'That's all right.'

'You want it or you don't?'

'I'll take it. Thank you.'

Reaching into his pocket, the bartender smiled as if he'd just lost a silly game but felt sure the outcome would have been different if the rules had been properly explained. He drew a cigarette from his pack with a little flourish before placing it on the counter in front of me. It was still there when he returned a few minutes later with my Martini.

'Sorry,' he said. 'It's busy this evening.'

'I wasn't aware of the wait.'

The bartender smiled again and lowered his voice. 'Lots on your mind? We don't have many patrons like you – I hope you don't mind if I say this.'

'I suppose it depends what you mean by "like me".'

'You know *Nighthawks*? The famous American painting? You have a bit the look of this man. The same nose, dark suit.'

'But no redhead next to me.'

The waiter shrugged in a manner that suggested my response if anything lent substance to his observation. 'Usually here it's families, tourists. The West End crowd.'

'Where in France are you from?'

'Champagne – like the drink! And you?'

'I know the Champagne region a little.'

'Perhaps you have made a tour of the vineyards? These can be quite interesting.'

'No, I have friends who live there.'

A middle-aged couple came and stood rather near me, I thought, considering there was otherwise plenty of space along the bar. The wife or more likely girlfriend was closest; a discreet glance revealed she was at least a decade younger than her companion. She seemed nervous, holding tight to the rail of the bar as if we were on an ocean liner during a rough sea-crossing. Wafts of Cinzano came off her. The pair gave the impression of having run out of conversation a while ago and I was tempted to reassure the woman that her date was almost certainly a bore and that wasn't something she could accept any blame for, unless one were talking in the wider sense of her life choices until this point. Instead I said nothing, merely felt her stare greedily at the cigarette lying on the counter.

The barman ignored them. 'British? Americans?'

'A local family.' By local I meant their ancestors were castellans back in the twelfth century and their name adorned rows of bottles behind the barman. Even if I'd been trying to impress the Frenchman I wouldn't have told him this, since I knew – the thought depressed me – that in vaguely sensing I was holding back on some grand connection he was more intrigued than if I'd referred to it.

After the champagne margaritas and the whiskey sour and now the Martini I was starting to feel a little woozy. It was not intelligent preparation, even if I was not entirely clear what exactly I was preparing for. Did I intend to reason with Héctor? To surprise him? To *attack* him? I had no weapon. And even if I did, and had avoided alcohol all evening, my training in that sort of thing was probably too long ago to be of any use.

There was a degree of fatalism as well as recklessness in my plan, if one could call it that. It simply felt preferable to waiting for Héctor to tell Antonia everything about my past, assuming he hadn't done so already; or to try framing me for Diana's murder; or come for me with a knife. This way I was at least exerting some form of control over events, not to mention cutting short the pleasure I knew the Mexican was taking in my current disturbed state.

It was approaching midnight. Emboldened slightly by drink I decided to do a circuit of the park. I'd strolled through it many times in the past, but made an effort now to memorise the topography. It was not a large area: fifty or sixty acres at most. With the Ritz at one end and Buckingham Palace at the other the neighbourhood could hardly be called seedy. Nor did the park appear to be a cruising ground. Despite the advantage of remaining open all night it was too small for that sort of thing, and I could see the

149

shaded dips and bushes were insufficiently private. Though I supposed one couldn't rule out the convenience of the location if a bored Arab hotel guest or drunken Russian stumbling out of Novikov lacked the wherewithal to find somewhere more suitable.

Trampling across the sodden lawns, taking in the bland lime and oak trees, and the complete absence of flowers (*pace* the vanished spring daffodils), it was hard not to conclude that of all the royal parks this one had the least to recommend it. Even the war memorials seemed either half-hearted or clunkily sentimental.

I'd finished my tour of the perimeter. Near the park's main entrance the hireable deckchairs had been packed away for the night, and the Italian teenagers were nowhere to be seen. The only sign of life was a single maintenance contractor trundling down the concrete path in a buggy.

Back on Piccadilly I turned right to the arcade, with its famous bulb-lit lettering. 'Good evening, Mr Hoffer,' beamed Ma, the Tongan doorman who had once chatted to me unself-pityingly about the knee injury that finished his professional rugby career.

Inside the Ritz, instead of heading for the Rivoli Bar I went up to the reception desk and asked for a room. 'Overlooking the park, if that's possible.'

'We have a deluxe suite,' the receptionist said, her voice sweetly innocent, but with the good grace not to lift her eyes from the computer screen.

I tried to blank the cost from my mind. 'Can I smoke up there?'

'It's a non-smoking room. I'm afraid if you do there'll be a charge.'

150

'That's all right.'

'Would you like me to send up an ashtray?'

'And some matches, please.'

'Of course, Mr Hoffer. We also have a selection of cigars and pipe tobacco.'

'Just the matches will be fine. Thank you.'

The sitting room of the suite reminded me of a smaller version of the Turners' house: all cream and gold leaf and Louis Seize chintz under a too-large chandelier. In the minibar I found a small and no doubt wildly expensive bottle of whisky. I'd drunk too much this evening but had a macabre sense that I ought to take little pleasures where I found them. For the same reason – I'd demanded the cigarette from the bartender impulsively, surprising myself – I opened the window and, staring out at the greenish-black murk, smoked for the first time in decades.

Afterwards I folded and hung up my suit and went through to the bedroom, where I lay on the king-size bed with my arms on my chest like a vampire. There was no need to ask reception to give me a wake-up call in a couple of hours. I wasn't going to sleep.

Mayfair loomed grandly behind the line of trees. After all these years I was still surprised by the coolness of London's night air, which even a heatwave remarked on to the point of mild obsession could not dislodge. The park was silent and felt larger and more shadowed than a few hours ago. I walked at what I hoped was a confident unhurried pace toward Constitution Hill, where a lunatic shooter had once tried to assassinate Queen Victoria. The occasional passing black cabs with their orange 'taxi' lights illuminated both reassured and tempted me.

I continued this latest lap of the park, along the hill and then round past the perfunctory pillars of the Memorial Gates, feeling groggy and also rather ridiculous, as if this were one of those unsettling situations one knew one would later laugh about when recounting it to friends. Though of course I would not do that. There was no sign of Héctor or anyone else, including my jowly follower from Kensington and later the train platform. I began nevertheless to feel exposed wandering around in this fashion, and it was with my nerve somewhat deserting me that I took cover inside the Bomber Command Memorial.

This most recent of the park's memorials was an open-top temple. Like its imposing Doric columns, the marble and Portland Stone evoked, in seeming rebuke of my present mood, classical virtues of strength and nobility. I leant beside one of the wall-mounted bronze torch-holders. Behind me, the memorial temple opened directly onto Piccadilly and I could hear the infrequent whoosh of vehicles descending into an underpass.

At the centre of the temple the statues of bomber pilots resembled oversized toy figurines. I thought of my half-brother, downed somewhere over Korea in possession of a Distinguished Service Cross and graceful pitching arm. Or so I'd gleaned from the slurred talk of uncles. My father never referred to him and my mother was not his mother, the famously alluring *mexicana* of Fairfield County. (In another version, she was from Texas and part Cherokee; the part about her looks didn't seem to be in dispute.)

152

Someone was approaching. In my pocket I felt for my Yale door key and slipped this jagged end first between my third and fourth finger. I closed my fist. Seconds passed. I listened intently to the approaching steps, which had a particular rhythm, a sort of scraping shuffle, and was surprised by the fleeting sense of disappointment when I relaxed my fingers and let the keys spill from their grip in my pocket.

It was the boy, Dorian Hamilton.

17

His formerly sleek gelled hair was now a mess of seaweedy black clumps. The look on his face was both sheepish and defiant.

What did he think he was doing, I demanded to know, following me around at this hour? I was growing a little tired of these troubled children mutely presenting themselves before me.

'I wasn't *following* you.'

Even in the darkness I could see his jaw was clenched, and that his temples and the base of his throat glistened from sweat as well as rainwater. His knee must have ached from all the walking he'd done this evening.

'Dorian.'

The boy heard the note of resignation in my voice because he seemed to relax slightly. 'Okay,' he said, 'maybe I was a little. But you *did* bolt from the room just as Lady Antonia was coming over to speak to you – everyone saw it. I was worried about you.'

'If that's true I don't see why you didn't catch up with me after I left Belgravia Square.' I glanced at Dorian's bow-shaped leg, the heel slightly raised from the pavement, like a dog with an injured paw. 'What I mean is you didn't need to skulk around Pall Mall and Piccadilly all this time, getting soaked. It's been *hours*! Without question you'll wake up with a fever tomorrow.'

He shrugged. 'I didn't think you were going to stay the whole night at the Ritz – why would you, when you live like fifteen minutes away? I waited for ages but then my knee got sore. I was about to leave when suddenly there you were, heading into the park. And then I *had* to keep following you!' he said with a grin. 'Who wanders around Green Park at past three in the morning?'

'You should go home immediately.'

Behind us the statues of the Bomber Command crew were illuminated by mounted spotlights. Staying in the temple shadows, careful to conceal myself as much as possible behind a pillar, I peered out at the lawn, which was black apart from the weakly lamplit main paths. The only noise came from the odd car or night bus on Piccadilly.

'If you're in some sort of trouble,' Dorian said, 'maybe I can help you.'

'If you really mean that—'

Shiny-eyed: 'I do!'

'Then you'll get a cab back to Little Venice.'

'Has this got something to do with that Mexican guy? The one with the scar?'

Faintly at first, once again I heard footsteps approaching. This time the walker's movements were regular and assured – the smooth clipping of the Berluti heels against the concrete path suggested their owner was not concerned to hide his arrival.

I saw with belated certainty that Itai's motives in encouraging this encounter were not altruistic. With a finger to my lips, I silently indicated the exit behind us, which led on to Piccadilly. Then in an exasperated whisper: 'Go!'

'First tell me what he did. Or what he *is*?' Dorian said.

I grabbed Dorian's face, felt the smooth skin go taut. 'You were right about Roland – he's a vulture who takes you for an idiot. Accept the Russian offer. Go back to San Diego; see your mother.'

He pushed my hand away. I'd been holding his jaw tightly and was surprised by the firmness of his gesture. 'I'm not leaving,' Dorian said. 'This guy won't *hurt* me – he has no reason to. Anyway, he wouldn't dare. Don't I own a famous company?'

Héctor was a couple of paces from the memorial temple. We were hidden behind the pillar but he must have been able to hear our muffled voices.

'Dorian!' I hissed.

Perhaps because he was both tired and charged with adrenalin, or in spinning round he put too much weight on his aching knee, or the alcohol from earlier in the evening had left him unsteady; or perhaps – perhaps – it was only a small stumble but in attempting to grab him I applied some pressure to his back; but when he stepped out from the temple Dorian lost his footing.

It was a precipitous movement which, given the hour and otherwise silent park, would have seemed hostile to an oncomer. There followed a muffled collision of bodies and then a sound resembling a trowel being plunged into earth, followed by a dull thud.

I drew the umbrella like a javelin behind my ear. When Héctor came into the temple he was crouched as a hunter; his eyes were black voids and there was a single smear of

157

blood across his majestic Indian cheekbones. I could see he was trembling faintly. This was my chance, when his senses were briefly clouded by the pleasure of killing. Taking aim at his right eye-socket I drove the steel point of the umbrella into it as hard as I could.

He screamed in fury more than pain, and then the umbrella was flying and he sprung at me, his face a shiny mess. He was left-handed; the memory rose from my unconscious, or perhaps I simply grabbed an arm at random before catching sight of the wet blade at the end of it.

We were pressed against each other. I felt his hot animal breath, the trembling of my arm muscles – a screaming accumulation of lactate familiar from the swimming pool. *The eagle and the serpent*, I stupidly thought of our entwined bodies. Then he twisted away and my forearm felt as if it had been splashed with boiling water. With his now free knife-hand he swiped at air. I couldn't see the umbrella but knew it was behind me, just beyond the statues of the air-force pilots. We circled each other. I was careful to stay on the side of his mangled eye and when he sidled in front of the marble plinth I charged him, dropping my shoulder like a rugby player at the moment before contact. At first I wasn't sure whose skull produced the sickening cracking noise. I was aware only of the explosion in my right arm, which I'd thrown out to break my fall.

I rolled to my feet. It was then I saw the misalignment of the Mexican's forehead, and understood it had been caused by the edge of the plinth. In the next instant, like speeded-up footage of a blooming flower, a number of red dots appeared at the point of the fissure. They merged to form a line of blood, which proceeded to pour into his good eye. I ran to the umbrella and made to grab at it but my right arm had become heavy and unresponsive, and when my fingers closed round the handle and I tried to yank it upwards I felt another sharp pain. The umbrella fell to the ground.

Héctor was on his knees, swaying a little. Leaving the umbrella where it lay I went over and kicked him hard in the jaw. By now my Norton & Sons suit was drenched in sweat and the navy linen as well as the white dress shirt underneath was stuck to my right forearm. A police siren could be heard from somewhere; I couldn't immediately tell if it was heading in this direction.

I crouched next to Héctor.

'William . . .' he rasped almost tenderly. His face seemed to have been reimagined in some sort of awful Francis Bacon homage, and when he tried to get further words out it was from behind a curtain of gore. 'William . . .'

For my part there wasn't much to say. He didn't resist as I closed my fingers over his and eased the knife from his grip. Working fast (I was uncomfortably aware we were still under the memorial's spotlights) I moved round until I was kneeling behind his head. With a rather odd sense we were stage actors in a tragedy I tried awkwardly to hoist him by his armpits. I wanted him leaning forward so that the arteries in his neck were more anterior and easy to cut: he had already bled so much he must have been half-dead, but I needed to make absolutely sure. Without the proper use of my right arm I struggled to acquire enough leverage to raise his body, and after a few seconds I gave up. His head continued to loll backwards against my stomach, which meant the blood vessels in his neck had retreated into the muscle. There was nothing to be done about it. I cut in an arc,

159

commencing from under his right ear, but the resulting bleeding was like a gentle lapping wave and not the vigorous spray I'd wanted. In frustration and gathering panic I tossed the knife and let his head slide off my thighs to the floor. He lay there making gurgling sounds. I fetched the umbrella again. Raising it high with my left hand, planting my feet on either side of his shoulders, I brought the steel tip down again and again onto his neck until my arm was too sore to do it with proper force, but by then the task was accomplished.

I became aware of the oppressive silence of the park. At some point without me noticing the police siren must have receded into the distance. I checked my watch: a quarter to four. Stepping out of the memorial, my vision dimmed and I thought I would black out. Then it passed and I wiped the end of the umbrella on the grass and checked on Dorian. He had been stabbed through the heart – lifeless of course, with a frightened expression the memory of which I instantly suppressed by focusing on how I was going to get back to Onslow Square. There was obviously no question of returning to the Ritz now. Thankfully, I often settled my tabs at the Rivoli Bar at the end of the month, and given my long-standing custom I doubted they would be unduly alarmed if I hadn't paid the room bill by checkout time tomorrow morning.

The simplest plan – since I couldn't think of a *good* one, it would have to do – was to hail a car on Piccadilly. Certainly not a hackney carriage. I had in mind one of the unlicensed minicabs that were common enough at this time of night. My suit was badly stained, but in the dark there was a chance this wouldn't show up too much on a casual rear-view mirror inspection. I spat into my handkerchief and scrubbed vigorously at my hands and face. My arm was still bleeding but the adrenalin had sobered me up, and even looking a little pale or quite possibly green I was confident I could put on a calm enough demeanour not to arouse too much suspicion. If I kept the passenger window wound down to help with the dizziness and nausea – not to mention the salty-metallic stench coming off me – and made sure to tip the driver generously, there was a small chance I could manage the short journey back to Kensington. Beyond that was rather more doubtful, but I'd have to worry about that later.

Part IV

18

I woke to a throbbing pain in my arm and the sound of Agustina knocking on my bedroom door. My housekeeper was usually very respectful of my privacy. It was one of the main reasons she had lasted so long in my employment, together with her claim to possess only limited English – after the unlisted number, Agustina was my second line of defence against telephone callers – and a troubled visa situation. The last had seemed a useful bargaining chip should such a thing ever be needed, which happily had never yet been the case.

If our conversation rarely strayed beyond a carefully circumscribed range of subjects, what I most valued about Agustina was all the things she *didn't* feel the need to talk about, starting with my lack of discernible employment and tendency to retire to the bath for half the morning to drink gin and tonic and listen to Mozart. Then there was my occasional habit of vacuuming and polishing every inch of the flat mere hours after she had completed the same tasks. (This had nothing to do with her professionalism, which was exemplary.) Not to mention the syringes and neurotoxins in the bathroom – Agustina, with her noble Indian crags, was no more a user of Botox than Proust's

Françoise. Or the fact that, left to myself, I rarely ate breakfast or lunch, and might for weeks at a time purchase only thin slices of *bife de lomo* for my occasional free (that is to say, blessedly solitary) evenings. Or that I always asked her to tell phone callers I wasn't at home, unless the person trying to reach me was Russian, when I would ask her to hand me the receiver immediately.

Agustina's discretion made my routine – really my entire existence – possible. So much of my life was spent telling lies, or trying to remember which untruths I'd told whom, it was a great relief to know that when I came home I would never be required to invent anything, even if the price was scarcely saying anything at all.

It concerned me to think the situation might be about to change. Possibly my housekeeper's present out-of-character acts of disturbance, her door-rapping and tentative *¿Señor Hoffers?*, were merely a reflection of my own unusual behaviour. After all, even on my most leisurely days I was never still in bed at half-past ten.

My mind however couldn't help racing. Had the Metropolitan Police arrived? Livid Mexican officials? Livid *Russians*? Perhaps there were bloodstains somewhere in the flat that I'd missed when cleaning up a few hours ago.

From where I lay in bed I could see the ruined suit and umbrella. (Not that to the naked eye there was anything necessarily incriminating about the umbrella, which I'd washed thoroughly before falling into an uneasy sleep around dawn. While the metal shaft was now bent out of shape, so that the wooden handle curved at an angle, this sort of minor structural damage was common for reasons other than destroying a person's jugular. All things considered, the brolly was as resilient as one would expect of an item loaned by the Imperial Club.) Beneath both those items was Héctor's blade, which I'd taken with me from Green Park.

There were little red dots on my bed sheets. I would need to change the bandage on my arm, though I was pleased to see the staining on the dressing was limited. A few hours ago Vicodin had mostly numbed the pain as I cut away where the shirt and jacket had become adhered to my flesh, and then slowly peeled the blood-caked cotton and linen from my right arm. On inspecting the wound I realised I was going to be left with a long, disfiguring scar; that I was going to feel self-conscious of this in the swimming pool; and would need to invent some story about how I acquired it. Having cleaned the cut as best I could with antiseptic wipes, and taken a steadying gulp of Japanese whisky – an old gift I found at the back of my drinks cabinet with the bottle's seal still unbroken; it seemed a waste to choose anything really decent – I'd begun the painstaking procedure with the needle and thread.

'*Dígame*,' I called to Agustina, still outside my bedroom door. I carefully manoeuvred my arm into my dressing-gown sleeve as she explained that *Señor* Roland Turner had called three times already this morning. On each occasion he'd said it was an urgent matter and he needed to speak to me immediately. (Proof that Agustina could understand English perfectly well, and it suited her as much as me to pretend otherwise.) What should she say if he called again?

'*Dile que no me siento bien. Lo llamaré mañana.*' I told her to convey the same message regarding my ill health to anyone else who telephoned or arrived at the door, no

167

matter how urgent they claimed their business was. No, I didn't need anything from the *farmacia*; thank you, I was fine without a home visit from a doctor or nurse. (For a moment I was tempted to agree to the last suggestion, if only to make use of the expensive private healthcare I'd purchased shortly after meeting Nikolai. But it wasn't worth the risk of having to explain to a medical professional what had caused my injury.) I ended the conversation with Agustina by telling her I intended to sleep, and since I therefore wished the flat to be silent she should take the rest of the day off.

What I really needed to do was dispose of the suit and umbrella and knife, only somehow I couldn't rouse myself to the task. It was more than physical exhaustion and the dull ache from my arm. I felt at once invulnerable (from the painkillers and – the distasteful truth of it – cutting a man's throat) and hollowed out. This odd condition left me reluctant to leave my bedroom or even remain conscious, if it could be helped.

At last I heard Agustina's slippers padding down the corridor. I took another couple of Vicodin and another slug of whisky; I'd sleep for just a few hours, and on waking deal with the incriminating objects. Reapplying the bandage on my arm was something else that would have to wait until later. I lay on my back with the tender forearm carefully positioned on my chest. My last thought before sinking back into sleep was that the Yamazaki single malt was surprisingly good.

19

I was at a street party on Havana's *Malecón*. Ingy Vowles was there, complaining about everything: the ghastly tinny salsa and the fat Cuban women in their colourful Lycra and the melting ice cubes in her mojito, which were giving her a terrible stomach ache. We were swept up in some sort of American tour party, which included people I hadn't seen for years, old faces from West Point and before. Teddy Wasserman. Gus Miller. The locals began jeering at us. '*Putos gringos*,' one of them shouted. Another had a custom-made Kramer knife; I knew from the distinct chevron patterning on the blade it was mine and he'd stolen it. Teddy Wasserman got pulled into the crowd. He reached out a hand as he was swallowed up and I saw the panic in his eyes but there was nothing I could do for him. When I tried to move my arm I discovered it had been slashed and I felt faint from the bleeding. Then I was in Brooklyn, or the Brooklyn of the American realist style: fire hydrants and denim skies, brownstone and late August heat. I wandered the deserted pavements searching for Antonia Highclere. The problem – it was, distinctly, a problem – was that I couldn't remember the name of the restaurant where we'd arranged to meet. It was a broiling afternoon; sweat poured off my body, making great blooming stains on my blue dress shirt. Eventually I found her in a lamplit place in a fur-lined coat drinking a Negroni. The cool russet interior was full of patrons who watched as the maître d' led me to a central table. She was looking in another direction but I knew she was calmly furious, that her energies henceforth would be devoted to harming me, and this knowledge despite the chill of the room made me perspire more. I woke as she turned to face me.

'*El Señor Turner quiere hablar con usted.*'

'Tell him I'm still unwell,' I called out in Spanish, trying to master my grogginess and panic. I had no sense of what time of what day it was. Before passing out I'd miraculously remembered to wind my watch ('We wouldn't normally recommend spending that sort of sum repairing an Omega,' the man in Bond Street sniffed, when I presented him with my brother's timepiece) and saw now that I'd been asleep for almost twenty-four hours. 'I'll call him tomorrow.'

'*No está en el teléfono. ¡Está aquí – en el apartamento!*'

'He's here?' Roland had never visited my flat before.

'*Sí, señor.*'

I told Agustina to send him away, an instruction she acknowledged with a note of surprise. It must have seemed to my housekeeper that I'd acquired some strange habits recently: rudely addressing her through closed doors; paying her not to come to work; declaring myself – I who was so proud of my good health, who was strangely impervious to the winter colds that struck down half of London – too ill to leave my bed. At least she wouldn't have trouble ascribing this refusal to see visitors to vanity, if my physical condition rendered me less than completely presentable.

Roland's indignant voice boomed through the flat. More than ever I was grateful for Agustina's convincingly dubious English and Incan resolve. He was not getting past her, though I didn't intend to risk leaving my bedroom just yet.

While I waited for them to leave I gathered my thoughts. Among other things Roland's presence here meant he'd found out about Dorian's murder, which implied it was in the news. Perhaps Roland had already been interviewed by the police and was here to warn me of something.

Or accuse me. My sense of invincibility after killing Héctor was by now in firm retreat. And I was puzzled why I myself hadn't yet been questioned or even arrested by Scotland Yard. Almost a day and a half had passed since the pair of bodies had been left, like sacred offerings, at the memorial temple.

The most immediate way the discovery of the corpses could lead back to me was if there had been any witnesses at Green Park, or if there were some other means of placing me there at the relevant time. *Had* anyone seen the killings? The fight with Héctor seemed to go on forever, but in fact the whole sequence can't have taken longer than two or three minutes. The period in which we were in the glare of the memorial spotlights would have been a fraction of that time: perhaps twenty or thirty seconds in total.

Thanks to the earlier storm and lateness of the hour I'd been sure we were alone in the park – though whether I could entirely trust in my vigilance was another matter. I recalled looking out for my jowly phantom. But during the struggle with Héctor I hadn't registered the receding of

171

the police siren, so there was clearly a period when I was incapable of focusing on anything other than the immediate danger of his knife. Nor had I spotted Dorian trailing me earlier in the evening.

Another worry was a pedestrian on Piccadilly passing the memorial entrance at an inopportune moment. If there had been such a person, however, and if he or she had reported something suspicious, I was certain the location was so central that the police would have arrived by the time I was climbing into the meter-less minicab at Hyde Park Corner. Besides – would a witness have inevitably alerted the authorities? (I had to hope the Somalian cab driver wouldn't risk his black-market job by reporting any suspicions about his bloodied passenger.) In that respect it was fortunate the Bomber Command Memorial was at the quieter end of Piccadilly. Someone walking to or from Park Lane or Knightsbridge in the early hours of a weekday, after a dramatic thunderstorm, was not necessarily, I thought, doing so for morally scrupulous purposes that he or she wouldn't mind making public via the police.

That still left passengers in cars or night buses to consider. Travelling at thirty-ish miles an hour – a little more, probably, at that time of night – they could have got at most a glimpse of me before the view was obscured by the memorial pillars. Anyone driving would have had even less time. To see what? Two middle-aged men in tailored suits engaged in some sort of drunken tussle . . . Which was not to say a person inclined to dismiss this strange tableau might not subsequently come across a media report of the murders, and then decide to dial 999.

And even if, by some miracle, no civically minded citizen saw the fight and proceeded to contact the police, CCTV was ubiquitous in London. Perhaps I was in luck and the park and memorial side of Piccadilly were not monitored by cameras. But Pall Mall? Piccadilly Circus? The Ritz?

It would not be long before the police established I was the only person at the Mexican embassy party who knew both Héctor and Dorian. What was more, my impulsive grab of the young man's jaw meant my fingerprints were on at least one of the dead bodies. A half-competent inspector would look for – and quickly find – social connections between the missing Mexican schoolgirl and her murdered compatriot. No doubt Diana had schoolmates at the Lope de Vega whose parents either worked as diplomatic staff at the Mexican embassy or knew people who did.

At trial I could plead self-defence regarding Héctor, though given the nature and extent of his injuries it would be hard to argue I'd employed reasonable force. In any case, it would hardly matter. Quite apart from whatever charges the Crown Prosecution Service brought against me for Comala and Diana, and perhaps even Dorian, thanks to the latter's friend Edwin I knew that American journalists had plenty of material about my past lives, my work for Nikolai and other Russians and my connections with the British establishment. If the Americans had a file on me, so would the local media.

As far as the Ingys and Rolands and (above all) Antonias were concerned, it was one thing for a person to be the subject of exotic rumour, quite another for certain cold facts to be aired. Becoming an outcast meant the final collapse of my precarious finances, which in turn would leave me friendless and – by the time the Home Office was finished with me – quite possibly stateless.

In the hallway the foghorn protestations had ceased. I could hear Agustina slowly putting away cleaning materials; probably she was taking her time to avoid sharing the small lift with Roland. At length I heard the front door close.

My arm was aching again. Any pressure on it or sudden movement produced a wave of pain. It was clear that without proper medical treatment and physiotherapy the damaged muscles wouldn't heal, meaning there would be no need after all to invent a plausible locker-room story for the scar. I wouldn't be swimming again.

Gingerly, I got out of bed and eased into my dressing gown. The phone on my writing desk began to ring. I had no intention of answering it. In the en suite bathroom, where I'd gone to re-bandage my arm, I found myself staring at the open medicine cabinet and more particularly its array of painkillers. There were plenty of Vicodins left. Ignoring these, I reached for the Tilofyl. I consumed four tablets before returning to my bedroom and fetching the Yamazaki bottle.

With the aid of the whisky I swallowed another couple of Tilofyl. The phone went silent at some point while I was inspecting sachets of diamorphine powder. Almost idly I remembered I was meant to be formulating a plan to dispose of my bloodstained suit and other objects. Objects of vice, I thought rather dizzily.

A few minutes later I was injecting the opiate solution – it was not a quick procedure; pressing too hard on the syringe with the thumb of my injured arm made me feel

174

faint – when I heard knocking at the front door. Perhaps Agustina had departed at last, only to forget her keys? I went back to slowly plunging the syringe. The pain of the act and its instant reward made a curious contrast, but soon everything was pleasantly dimming. I thought of a line from Baudelaire: *La douceur qui fascine et le plaisir qui tue.*

My attention had returned to the Japanese whisky just as the knocking started up again. It was not especially loud or aggressive, but nonetheless there was an insistence to it, which even in my drifting state I found hard to ignore.

In the mirror there were dark yellowish pouches under my eyes. The unchanged bandage was beginning to give off a ripe saline smell. I hadn't washed or shaved or even brushed my teeth in over a day, and my breath was sour and oaky from the single malt.

A longish silence followed in which it seemed that Agustina, or whoever it was, had given up and left. I was contemplating another ten or twenty milligrams – or forty, why not? – of diamorphine, perhaps with a glass of ice-cold vodka, when the feline rapping started up again.

'William, it's me. Please open the door.'

Travelling four floors up to my flat was against Mrs Belsey's strict medical instructions to stay off her feet as much as possible. What made the visit all the more surprising was that she never made unannounced visits. In fact, aside from a yearly rather stilted sherry while John was alive, I couldn't remember her setting foot inside the premises in all the time I'd been her tenant.

'You're not answering your telephone! I spoke to your cleaning lady this morning,' she said – through the door I could feel her sense of purpose building. 'She claims you're unwell . . .'

The choice of verb was rather ominous.

'Whatever your condition, I must speak to you immediately. I must speak to you,' she repeated, 'before I call the police.'

20

Since the heart attack Mrs Belsey's face had become a mask. The line of her mouth, already slanted from the original stroke, had hardened while the flesh around it inexpressively sagged. Her eyes, however, remained as lively as always, and now widened at the sight of me. Pretending not to have heard any mention of the police, I offered her tea or coffee (she declined both) and gently scolded her for negotiating the rickety little lift when I could have easily popped down to see her.

'You're not answering your telephone,' she said for the second time, her voice thick and accusing.

It was a bore, I explained, but I'd been struck down by a virus the last day or so. 'I'm sorry – you must have thought I'd abandoned you.' Had Annabel (the austere daughter, who I knew had made several resentful visits from Canterbury) been checking on her? I wasn't quite up to visiting the shops yet, but first thing tomorrow Agustina could pick up any prescriptions or other supplies.

Mrs Belsey replied coldly that she didn't need any help from me.

'Well, if you're sure . . .' I said, as genially as I could manage in light of a powerful wave of nausea.

I invited her to come through to the sitting room. After a few paces, which I tried to take as steadily as possible, I glanced over my shoulder only to discover her still standing in the little hallway. My present floating feeling made it hard to judge whether I'd spoken loudly enough for her to hear me. Rather than repeat myself, and thereby risk an outright refusal, I decided to continue to the other room as though it hadn't occurred to me she wouldn't follow. If there was going to be a scene I didn't intend to make it easy for her.

Finally, I heard her tentative steps behind me.

'I won't be staying long.'

As much as the words themselves it was the tone in which they were delivered – of a sharp-tongued headmistress who'd been at the drinks cabinet – which carried the unsettling hint of a threat. She waved away my help in lowering herself onto the settee.

'I'm very sorry to hear that,' I said, conscious my innocent pose was already wearing thin. 'But of course you should be resting as much as possible – the last thing I want to do is pass on this awful virus . . .'

With a heavy blink she seemed to dismiss my slightly manic babbling. Naturally I was wishing I'd been more restrained with the Tilofyl and diamorphine. If it hadn't been for Dorian's white heroin, the shock of all the opiate in my system would quite likely have already caused me to pass out on the newly oriental-rug-less floor.

For her part, I could see Mrs Belsey's resolve wavering a fraction. She hadn't anticipated my dogged refusal to take offence at her brusqueness. Nor, it was plain, did she find it easy to broach a scenario so firmly outside of her experience. I rather felt for her, obliged as she was to confront me in the aftermath of a frightening health episode, without the support of her worldlier husband who would surely have known exactly what to do.

'Mrs Belsey.'

'Judy,' she said reflexively.

'I thought perhaps you might have been wondering about the teenage girl who visited me recently.'

It was enough – the words poured forth.

'She is *missing*, William! I saw it on the television. It was only a short item, they flashed up the photo so quickly but I'm *sure* it was her. They said she was Mexican, and I remembered your goddaughter had a Spanish accent. At first I thought perhaps I was going mad. I couldn't understand why you wouldn't have mentioned anything about it. Why when you came to visit you weren't frantic with worry, instead of sitting there, day after day, calmly reading me those dull pieces from the *Telegraph*. It was as though you were choosing them on purpose – as though you were trying to bore me to death!'

'I would like to explain everything,' I said, after a short oppressive silence. 'But I'm afraid it's rather complicated. Would you excuse me for a moment?'

On the pretext of making myself some tea, I made an uncertain attempt to get to my feet before collapsing back into the chair.

Mrs Belsey rushed on, 'What I can't stop thinking about, and which makes me feel I have a terrible *duty* here, is the time you and Antonia Highclere visited me at the hospital.'

179

'I may be wrong,' I said rather hoarsely, 'but as I recall we didn't arrive together.'

'I know perfectly well', she snapped, 'that she came separately. If you're implying my memory is confused.'

'Not at all,' I said, though it was precisely my suggestion.

'We spoke about Wimbledon, or rather Antonia did. She'd arrived directly from Centre Court. At one point the colour drained from your face and you repeated a remark she'd only just made, as if you hadn't really been listening. At the time I was rather distracted myself, but in retrospect I think it was unusual behaviour coming from *you*. Even so, it probably wouldn't have stayed in my mind, except Antonia noticed it too.'

From the way she delayed this little bombshell I wondered if my visitor was starting almost to enjoy herself. 'Antonia? What did she say exactly?'

Mrs Belsey was not going to be hurried. 'She came back the next day. You'd just gone for a swim, I think. Perhaps she was slightly disappointed about that. Anyway, she didn't stay long. At one point she said how charmingly old-fashioned you were. And so unaccustomed to modern televisions that when you spotted the news item about a missing Mexican girl you became distracted as a child. It was a casual and I suppose' – reluctantly, squirming – 'affectionate remark. Only, as with you, one has the impression Antonia Highclere always chooses her words—'

'What did you say?'

'To what?' she said, startled by my urgency.

'To her remark about me and the item on the news – about the Mexican girl.'

180

'I told her . . .' Her eyes closed in a rather satisfied manner. 'I told her that at the time I hadn't actually looked up at the screen. Even a little thing like that would have felt rather an effort during those days in the hospital,' she said parenthetically, as though I hadn't been present at the time and seen for myself, 'and I've never been interested in tennis. Then I mentioned – really just for something to say – that I'd only recently known you had a Hispanic goddaughter.'

'Perhaps Antonia was surprised by this remark.'

'Oh yes! She was most interested to know the details of my encounter with the girl, and what precisely she looked like. Though of course – you know this, William – Lady Antonia has a way of making one feel that *everything* one says is enormously fascinating. In this case the significance of her curiosity didn't dawn on me until I got home and finally saw the news for myself. I realised I'd described to her the very same Mexican girl on the television.'

At some point while Mrs Belsey was speaking the room had started to rotate. The last time I experienced something similar had been in a *cantina* in Oaxaca, the sort of place where the urinal by the bar was not a Duchampian whimsy.

My landlady's hands were knotted in her lap and she'd turned her face to the window. 'It was John who enjoyed watching Wimbledon.'

In profile her features showed no sign either of the old stroke or the recent coronary attack. Her melancholic grace in that instant made me think of the portrait of his mother Whistler completed at Cheyne Walk, not far from where we were sitting.

'He never liked you, you know. I'm talking about John. Your little English gentleman act might have worked on a few rich foreigners, but we could never imagine how you thought it could fool *us*.'

Her throat bulged and settled. I was reasonably certain she'd never in her life spoken so frankly to anyone, including her husband.

'Well,' I said, quietly. I was aware of smiling faintly. 'In summary . . .' Mrs Belsey, still staring out the window, gave no indication she was listening. 'In summary,' I repeated, 'I think what you'd like to know is whether I have any information about the whereabouts of the Mexican girl claiming to be my goddaughter. The one who went missing shortly after you gave her the keys to my flat.'

She returned her gaze to me and I saw in a moment of sharp embarrassment that the hard slope of her mouth revealed quite clearly the repulsion I inspired. The surly resolve had vanished, however.

Somewhat tremulously, she said, 'In fact I would far prefer *not* to know about any of it. But in the circumstances I feel compelled to ask what exactly your relation to this girl was – is,' she corrected herself. '*Do* you know anything about her disappearance?'

'You're asking', I said, 'if I murdered her.'

Though my focus was chiefly on managing not to vomit or lose consciousness, it was plain she was becoming upset.

'Oh, William!' she cried. 'What is this? What is happening?'

In a slightly pitiless tone I responded, 'I'm just trying to understand what you intend to accuse me of. When you call the police, I mean.'

'The police? I didn't say—'

'Ah, but I feel sure you did mention that, rather loudly when you were knocking on my door a moment ago.' I interrupted her whimpering to insist she wasn't to worry about explaining herself, that in fact it was *I* who'd promised *her* a full account of the situation. In as level a tone as I could muster I explained that Diana Domínguez Saavedra was the daughter of Rafael, an old acquaintance of mine from when I lived in Mexico. He was an engineer by profession but also, putting it simply, a money-launderer for drug traffickers. It seemed Rafael had become greedy and taken some of these illicit funds for himself. Realising not only he but quite possibly his daughter were now in some trouble, he'd advised Diana to come and find me at Onslow Square. Although it was unclear what he thought I could do to protect her, I warned Diana that she was in danger, and in particular she should avoid an official at the Mexican embassy here in London who I knew to be in the pay of the mentioned drug traffickers. Also an extortionist and murderer. 'In case of an emergency,' I explained, 'I let her keep your key to the flat.'

Mrs Belsey's bony fingers were at her temples. 'Stop it,' she said. 'I can't hear this.'

'A week or so later I returned from a party at the Tate to find Diana in the sitting room. Her throat had been cut.'

'Please,' she moaned. 'Stop.'

'I called a Russian businessman I know who has some experience of these matters, albeit not usually in this country. His associates came and removed the body. Also my oriental rug and an old throw I was rather fond of. There's a stained patch beneath where you're sitting where the wood is especially dark. My sharp-eyed housekeeper hasn't yet discovered it, though as you can imagine this hasn't stopped me scrubbing at it rather feverishly in the early hours.'

It wouldn't be long before Agustina spotted the stain and realised I'd slightly shifted the position of the settee to conceal it. Perhaps I'd tell her my 'virus' had caused me to faint, in the process cutting my forehead on the edge of the coffee table. All it required was a little nick to my temple followed by a couple of stitches – I was getting quite practised at using a sewing kit with my left hand.

'I couldn't simply go to the police,' I continued over her quiet sobs. 'Or rather I could have, but not without ruining my reputation, the life I've spent the last twenty years building.'

Perhaps it was the relief of unburdening myself – unlike Gianni Bardoni, I'd never formally confessed my sins – but the combined effects of the drugs and whisky seemed to have reached a peak, and I began to imagine over the next few hours slowly reasserting control over my poisoned system. The satisfaction this thought gave me was surprising: before Mrs Belsey's arrival I was fairly sure I had not intended to stop working through the collection of narcotics in the bathroom.

'You're probably wondering where this leaves things with Diana's murderer. Héctor Comala is his name, or was. We were actually rather close at one point, until I had a change of heart. But that was in another country,' I said with a wry smile. I was unsure myself whether I'd meant to echo *The Jew of Malta*, though fortunately I grasped the tawdriness of adding that the wench was dead.

Mrs Belsey was halfway to standing up when her arm seemed to slip or give out and she fell back awkwardly against the hard rest of the settee.

'It seems to be your turn to have trouble getting to your feet,' I said. 'But I was talking about Héctor. Oddly enough, I used the tip of an umbrella – it was what I had to hand; the whole murder was more or less spontaneous. I won't go into the details. What I do regret is that a confused young man also ended up dead. He wasn't supposed to be there.' At this point I probably looked rather beseechingly at Mrs Belsey, who had succeeded in rising from the settee. 'I tried to warn him, you see . . .'

Her fingers fluttered briefly to her kidney area, which must have been sore from the fall; then they were splayed in front of her as if she'd been plunged into darkness. In this unbalanced fashion Mrs Belsey stumbled towards the hall-way. A strangled yelp accompanied the tumbling of my new bronze skeleton from a side table. She lingered for a moment, battling a mad practical urge to reach down and inspect the little memento mori for any damage, but in the event recovered herself and lurched onwards. 'No! Oh, no!' she was repeating to herself.

At the front door she fumbled with the lock, and I was on the verge of catching up with her. The sight of my outstretched hand – too late, I felt the twinge from my damaged arm-muscle – seemed to spur her on. She threw open the front door with surprising force. I swivelled thoughtlessly, ensuring the door's hard edge made contact with the line of home-made stitches in my forearm. The pain distracted me for a moment or two. Meanwhile the door had swung shut. With my left hand I tried awkwardly to turn the lever while pressing the release button of the door lock.

When I eventually emerged onto the landing I expected to find my landlady already shuttered inside the lift, which was why I almost tripped over her. She was on her back staring at the ceiling, her eyes oddly unfocused.

I called her name with modest urgency. Her mouth was hanging open in rather undignified fashion. I considered closing it, but for all I knew that was premature and inside her frail chest she was frantically trying to draw breath. Hunched on my knees, leaning over her, I said, 'Judy?'

In the instant she grabbed my hand I couldn't stop myself from flinching. Quickly regaining my composure, I squeezed her palm comfortingly and met her beseeching gaze. At one point she managed a few words, but they were too garbled to make out.

21

It was Thursday evening, warm. I was listening to a Beethoven quartet with the window open, mentally planning a trip to Florence. There was a certain contrarian pleasure in visiting during high summer, when the city was stiflingly hot and so abandoned by the locals even the cinemas were closed. The snaking queues of tourists outside the Uffizi and Accademia were admittedly not appealing; but once one got the hang of Italian bureaucracy, it was easy enough (if not especially cheap) to obtain a cultural pass granting VIP access to virtually all of the city's galleries and churches. Then there were the jazz evenings at Santissima Annunziata, Bizet in the Boboli Gardens, lazy morning coffees in Santa Croce watching for Lucy Honeychurches with their Miss Bartletts. The bored tailors at the Ferragamo palazzo who, finally having something to do, took extra care to get the cut of my new suits just right.

As far as my life in London was concerned, my plan was simply to carry on as normal, or as near to that as possible. By the time the two women police officers visited me – 'just to tick all the boxes' – the knife and ruined suit were at the bottom of the Thames.

The younger officer had several closed-up ear piercings and said nothing the entire visit. Reluctantly, she held up the bronze skeleton while I pointed to the scuffing on the statuette's ebony pedestal where Mrs Belsey had knocked it to the floor. ('I blame myself. She was obviously very weak – I should have insisted on walking her to the lift. The thing was that, even when frail, she could be something of a force of nature . . .') When I casually mentioned the statuette had belonged to Yves Saint Laurent the poor girl almost dropped it herself.

Her senior colleague showed greater self-possession. Thirtyish, with the high forehead of a Velázquez *menina*, she had a watchful expression that put me on alert. In a brisk Estuary voice she passed on the reports from the hospital and, rather surprisingly, Mrs Belsey's daughter of my good citizenly conduct towards the deceased. (Annabel Belsey's generous words might have been partly motivated by guilt. She had lost no time in giving me written notice of her intention to sell my flat, along with her mother's, as soon as possible after they formally came into her possession.) Not quite convincingly, I felt, the *menina* officer thanked me for the support I'd provided Judy Belsey during the 'difficult period' between her first and second heart attacks, especially – both women's eyes now trailed to the discreet pair of stitches at my temple – given my own recent ill health. Neither of them appeared to notice the dark patch of floor beneath where they were sitting, which might in any case have been the shadow cast by the settee, or an old stain or feature of the wooden boarding.

'Would anyone like more tea?' I asked, though they hadn't touched their Earl Greys. (I claimed to be out of English Breakfast.)

Instead of accepting the hint the senior officer said, 'Apart from you and her daughter, it seems Judy didn't have any visitors when she returned from the hospital.'

'Well, she had *friends*,' I said stiffly. I felt oddly defensive for poor Mrs Belsey, who would have loathed this prying into her personal affairs. 'Or at least she was known in the neighbourhood. She lived here most of her life. The trouble is there are fewer English residents of Kensington these days, especially from her generation. As you may know, her husband died a couple of years ago.'

'She was lonely.' The officer regarded me thoughtfully. 'A bit isolated.'

'If she was, she didn't mention anything to me. My neighbour was rather old fashioned in that respect.'

'Landlady.'

'I'm sorry?'

'She was your landlady, wasn't she?'

'Yes, that's right.'

'Not merely your neighbour.'

'Is that what I said?'

'It was.'

The colleague scribbled something on a clean notepad.

'Then let the record stand corrected.'

Her humourless smile revealed brownish-grey teeth, the colour of salmon fat. 'You're not in court, Mr Hoffer. This is a very informal visit – if it helps, think of it as community support as much as law enforcement.'

'"As much as" or "instead of"?'

Another bland baring of teeth. 'It's not often someone passes away while visiting your flat.' I didn't point out it was becoming a more regular event than one might think.

Possibly she already had her suspicions. 'Sometimes,' she continued, 'people find they'd like someone to talk to, especially when they don't have partners or close friends . . .'

'Thank you for the offer,' I said, not excessively warmly.

With faux casualness the senior officer proceeded to mention that on their way up they had knocked at the other flats in the building. No one seemed to be in.

'That's not a surprise – the other residents live abroad most of the year.'

'But they could charge a fortune in rent! Why don't they find tenants?'

'Well, I don't think they need the money.'

She reflected on this for a moment. 'As I was saying, Judy Belsey must have felt isolated – on her own in this empty building.'

'I really wouldn't know; I suppose it's possible. Though I was here too, of course. She wasn't completely alone in that sense.'

'Of course, yes. But presumably you're at work a lot,' she ventured slyly.

'Are you sure neither of you would like more tea?'

The *menina* answered for them both with a brisk shake of the head. 'Can I ask what you do for a living?' she persisted.

'I'm an art consultant,' I said, hoping this would be sufficiently flummoxing. Again the younger officer wrote something on her pad.

'And it's just you here – you rent this flat by yourself?'

I smiled faintly. 'Were you wondering if I get lonely too?'

The officers coloured at the same moment. I was becoming anxious for the interview to be finished – all the more so when, in a tone of juvenile petulance, the *menina* replied that actually she sort of *was* wondering about that. 'Specifically, I wondered if you'd had any visitors in the last few weeks. Any female visitors.'

The mute officer glanced up at her colleague. Her expression – lasting a split-second before, her cheeks still aflame, she plunged her attention back to the pad in her lap – conveyed surprise and also a note of caution. The *menina* never took her gaze off me, but from the way her jaw clenched with irritation I knew she'd registered her junior partner's response.

'I'm a very private person,' I said. 'I hope you understand.'

'Oh, yes. Absolutely . . . !' She made an effort to say this invitingly, even furnishing me with a final hideous grin. It quickly faded. Whatever had prompted the younger policewoman's loaded glance it was clear that, on this occasion at least, I wasn't going to need to mention anything about calling my lawyer.

Naturally I was alarmed by this visit. I had no illusion the Leviathan, suspecting my connection with the 'disappearance' of Diana as well as (surely, given CCTV footage and so on) the confirmed deaths of Héctor and Dorian, planned to leave me alone indefinitely. But what purpose did a delay serve? There were moments when this question seized me and I felt I might vomit. The fear I was experiencing some sort of extended intermittent hallucination was reinforced by a further sighting of my jowly pursuer on my way to the newsagent the day before. It was reaching the point where he seemed quite brazenly to be tailing me almost every time I stepped outside the flat.

My immediate thought was this corpulent shadow worked in some way for the British state. But there were grimmer possibilities. Despite my strong intuition he was an Englishman, he could have been connected with the CIA or Nikolai, or even the Ortega cartel.

I finished my Aperol Negroni (I was out of Campari) and lit a cigarette. The smoking was a new development, in part bitter freedom of no longer needing to protect my swimmer's lungs. Probably the habit wouldn't last much longer than the first quizzical half-smile from Antonia. That was if she planned to speak to me again, given my rude flight from the Cartier party and the troubling information she had received from Mrs Belsey about my link to the missing Mexican teenager.

She often dined at Boone's on Thursdays. In many ways Antonia Highclere embodied the spirit of the restaurant. With its whitewashed walls and crisp table linens, abstract art and profusion of fresh flowers, the atmosphere was minimalist without quite lapsing into bland conservatism. It would never be unfashionable but one sensed that, as with Antonia, what Boone's represented was the more enduring quality of style. I also liked that it wasn't unusual to see patrons dining there alone, as I intended to do this evening.

The first person I saw on entering the restaurant was Gianni. He was horribly drunk, waving me over before I had the chance to make a swivelling exit.

'Guglielmo! Guglielmo – *vieni qui!*'

When hardly any diners in the busy room looked up I realised he must have been carrying on like this for a while.

He was with a conspicuously handsome fellow in his late twenties – a junior auctioneer, perhaps, or research student at the Courtauld, whose even features and look of saintly calm reminded me of Gustave Moreau's *The Young Man and Death*. The third and final member of the party, making my heart sink slightly, was Camilla Rhodes-Thorpe. I knew she didn't want me to join them, but in his present condition Gianni would never allow me to take a table by myself.

István, the Hungarian maître d'hôtel, was on the other side of the room listening to a French couple (they both seemed to be speaking at once) I vaguely recognised. When he saw me he made to excuse himself. I gestured to Gianni's table with a smile shading into a grimace, and he nodded and resumed his conversation.

'Come and meet your *paesano*! John Ford. Have you ever heard such a sublimely American name?'

The subject's frown suggested he was aware of the English playwright but had decided against saying anything.

'Oh, it's William,' Camilla said as I stooped to kiss her cheek. Her fragrance had been devised by a man she used in Jermyn Street, and its mandarin-cotton warmth was always a faint surprise. I remembered not to ask after Anders.

'Camilla's not eating,' said Gianni.

'He means I'm intruding,' Camilla clarified, since she was never seen to eat.

'You're waiting for friends?' – by which I meant Antonia.

With glazed pleasure Camilla said how odd it was I hadn't been invited. Harold was somewhere in Somerset, she added unnecessarily, since everyone except John Ford knew Harold wouldn't have come to dinner even if he were in Kensington. 'Apart from that I'm not too sure who's coming. I have a feeling it's mainly dancers and more bloody diplomats. Including of course' – an alarming smile – 'her new Mexican friend.'

'William is one of Lady Antonia Highclere's oldest *intimes* . . .' Gianni said, whether as pointedly as Camilla I couldn't decide.

'I think my boss went to dinner with her once.' The young American spoke with a cultured East Coast accent that matched or rendered superfluous the faint blue veins at his temple and wrists.

'Everyone,' said Gianni, 'has been to dinner with Antonia *once*.'

'Except for me it seems!' said the American.

I asked if he was with an auction house.

'A gallery, actually – just a small one.'

When Gianni supplied the name I replied I hadn't heard of it.

'You mustn't think William is a philistine. The truth is far more romantic: he's an exile.'

'You haven't been back to the States in a while?'

Again Gianni jumped in: 'Not for decades!'

The young man said he wasn't really surprised. In fact he might not have guessed I was a compatriot at all.

'Oh, I'm not sure we can let you claim him. At this point William is really *sui generis* – he of no nation.'

'Someone told me it was something to do with the CIA.' Camilla fixed me with a chilly glare. 'They got you your British passport—'

'That might not be exactly in their gift . . .' John Ford laughed good-naturedly.

'In return,' said Camilla, ignoring the young gallerist's interruption, 'for your agreement never to go back to America.'

Since she must have known how exhausting Gianni's reaction was going to be I was a little annoyed by this remark.

'To think of all those hours discussing Twombly and Rauschenberg! Those fripperies! When *of course* you're a spy, or some sort of fascinating double agent.' Having declaimed loudly in this manner Gianni clutched John Ford's arm. 'I'll need you to remind me of this in the morning.'

'I can do that,' said the young American, staring rather murderously at his gazpacho. 'At any rate if I see you.' He asked if I was interested in abstract expressionism.

'William is interested in *everything* – it's his great skill,' said Gianni.

'Everything and nothing. I've no idea where the others have got to, I must have written the time down wrong. What *is* the time, anyway?' Since Gianni was too gruesome and the boy too young, or she was oddly shy of his good looks, Camilla was obliged to address this question to her most recent object of insult.

I told her it was just coming up to nine. The waitress arrived – a lacrosse-shouldered summer hire, studying something or other at Exeter – and when he was finally satisfied he knew her father Gianni requested a bottle of champagne. I ordered veal, having barely glanced at the menu.

'I like your watch,' Camilla told me with an air of significant concession. Noticing my puzzled expression, she said

195

that for one thing it was not pathetically expensive. Everyone avoided looking at the Cartier on Gianni's wrist. 'Of course the pearl is faded, which makes it rather grimy-looking. Still, there's something oddly successful about it.' She took a thoughtful sip of wine. 'Maybe because it's sentimental, and that's the last thing one would expect of you.'

'Didn't Susan Sontag write somewhere,' John Ford began, boldly but unpromisingly, 'that at its most refined sexual beauty is like this? The subversive little detail, like the feminine lips of a macho movie star.'

After a short silence, Camilla said she didn't quite know how we had got on to talking about that sort of thing.

'I didn't mean to suggest any premeditation on Mr Hoffer's part.' The preppy blotches in the young gallerist's cheeks were now in bloom.

'Oh, I do hope there *was*,' said Gianni. 'I believe William might well be capable of such a touch of genius. To be maximally elegant and carnally desirable by means of a rather tattered old watch.'

'The truth is it belonged to my brother. I'm sorry to be a disappointment.'

Camilla wanted to know if he died tragically.

'I'm afraid he's quite alive, as far as I'm aware.'

'But he must have a *story*.'

'Not really. Mostly he drinks.'

Gianni gave me a quick appraising look. 'I thought your brother ran the nebulous Hoffer family enterprise.'

'Yes, that's right,' I said, surprised to discover that in some long-forgotten conversation he'd been paying attention after all.

*

196

Before my veal arrived Antonia Highclere came in with a group of young rajahs. Despite my jealousy I had to concede they looked effortlessly glamorous. Notable among them, in proud proximity to her elbow, was a Belarusian dance prodigy recently eulogised in the *FT* magazine.

'*There* you are,' Camilla said. 'By some awful mistake I've been here for hours. We were just talking about William's feckless brother.'

'I don't think I knew William had a brother,' Antonia replied, gracefully eliding any reference to this person's moral shortcomings. But she didn't invite me to join her table, not even for a quick aperitif or coffee after the meal, and when István led her party to the centre of the room I had the feeling of watching the great carnival roll on without me.

Minutes later Roland Turner showed up. He appeared to accept as quite natural the attention of the restaurant, even though the unusually stirred-up atmosphere owed rather more to the presence of the aristocrat ex-model and Slav ballet genius. As he marched straight past the table where Gianni and I were sitting I noticed an extra fixedness at his jaw which, for all his superficial confidence, hinted at great effort to master his nerves.

But if I was certain that, like me, Roland had come here this evening without concrete plans to dine with anyone in particular, the main clue was simply the situation in which he had latterly found himself. The privileged young luggage company heir found stabbed to death in Green Park had been receiving a lot of press coverage. Since facts about the crime itself were proving scarce, the one detail the papers had really seized on was 'City tycoon' Roland Turner bringing the young Hamilton to a VIP Cartier party on the evening of the murder. (To my surprise, there'd been no mention anywhere of Héctor Comala, or even of an unidentified second dead body.) Related speculation about Roland's interest in Dorian and even – in more veiled phrasing – his possible involvement in the boy's homicide was likely to give Antonia cause to reflect on their friendship. Not because the innuendo was lurid or even believable; it would have offended Antonia precisely because it was so absurd. Roland was in danger of looking fatally unserious.

It was bold of him to show up here as if this were any other Thursday. The stakes were high in as much as he would probably survive the press humiliation *if* Antonia chose now to greet him with her usual diffident charm. Again, not because she held such vertiginous sway in the beau monde, though she was certainly influential; it was more one thoroughly trusted her judgement, both of Roland's situation and of how her world would respond to it. Nor was it directly for Roland a question of commercial survival, even if for him more than most (but perhaps not me) much of his tireless socialising was by way of business. In any case, he evidently hoped that with Antonia's subtly communicated blessing he might now join her table as if he'd been invited all along.

'Some American just started bawling at me from inside his car. Wanting to know if this was the famous Boone's.' Roland was himself speaking at a fair volume. 'He seemed to think it unsporting of the restaurant not to employ a vulgar sign.'

'What did you tell him?' asked Camilla, incuriously.

'That I'd never heard of such a place, and glared till he roared off. Serves him right – shouting up the street as if he owns it. Someone with a driver and diplomatic number plates should be up to finding out where he's having dinner.'

The Lady was tilting her head at some impassioned whisper from the Belarusian. Despite her tolerant smile – Antonia didn't admire public displays of either passion or whispering – she seemed lost in private thoughts.

'You may have a point,' said Camilla, after glancing at Antonia, 'only one gathers he was meant to be dining with *us*.'

'Well then, I suppose it's fortunate I happen to be available to make up the numbers.'

At that moment the focus of the entire room seemed to move from the pair of empty seats at Antonia's table (the one reserved for Héctor, I, if no one else, was certain would remain unclaimed) to Lady Antonia Highclere herself. Even the now-silenced dancer, delightedly scanning the faces around him, sensed the prospect of some act of invisible violence.

In a voice all the more chilling for its lightness and reserves of sympathy, Antonia said, 'Roland, you're very welcome to join us. Of course you are! Only we don't want to steal you, if you were planning to join friends.'

'That's rather,' he said, 'what I had thought I was doing.'

Gianni, next to me: 'I can't bloody hear! Did Antonia just say . . .'

'Oh well,' she said, with smiling upper-class deliberation, in equal parts shy and unsparing, 'perhaps they're running late.'

The tycoon remained dreamily rooted, like a boxer in the moment before his body fully registered the deciding blow.

I stood up.

'Guglielmo, *ma cosa fai*? Leave the ghastly man to stew!' said Gianni.

A jagged line had appeared on John Ford's smooth forehead. He watched me with intense concentration, as if this were a scene from a difficult opera he'd like to be able to discuss. I smoothed my jacket and set off towards my stranded acquaintance.

'Roland, I've got a spot with Gianni Bardoni. We wondered if you'd like to join us.'

'Look who it is!' he sneered. 'Lazarus is risen for an evening at Boone's.'

A rajah *tsked* in half solidarity at Roland's rudeness.

'Your housekeeper was under the impression you were too ill to leave your bed. You look well enough to me, apart from that absurd cut above your eye.'

Neither Gianni nor Camilla had earlier bothered to enquire about the discreet pair of stitches on my forehead, or seemed to notice I was moving my right arm as little as possible. 'It's rather embarrassing. A dizzy spell from my virus. I fell and bumped my head.'

'Yes, well, anyway . . .' His wit had deserted him, and he opted inelegantly to wound. 'I see I'm not the only one banished from the top table. That's something at least.'

Camilla warned Roland, surely too late, that he was on the verge of being a terrible bore, while István showed his fabled professional sensitivity by hovering protectively near Antonia's chair.

'I've only just ordered,' I said calmly. 'Why not come and sit down.'

When Roland took a step towards me I could smell his sandalwood-and-*muguet* fury. 'Don't play the magnanimous gentleman with *me*!' The urge to crush my windpipe seemed to crystallise Roland's general opinion in my regard. '. . . You sordid prairie bootlicker!'

István's normally disguised Carpathian twang, like his self-doubting syntax, came through almost poignantly: 'Now, Mr Turner! I really must be asking you to leave.'

'Bumped your head, was it,' said Roland, ignoring the maître d' though sounding a fraction calmer. 'I do wonder if, instead of wasting their time hounding me, one of the fucking incompetents at the Metropolitan Police shouldn't establish what *you* were doing after the party last week.'

Gianni's protestations of *Basta!* – he didn't generally bother with Italian; I had the impression it was a bit of a performance for John Ford – further fuelled the high-dramatic atmosphere, which lingered even after Roland marched off in disgrace.

In the midst of all this Antonia addressed me with her usual quiet calm. 'William, are you sure you wouldn't like to join us?' she said, and it seemed for a moment she really was repeating an earlier offer. 'István can organise extra places for Gianni and his friend.'

'I think there's been enough disruption for one evening – but thank you.'

Camilla, taking her cue from Antonia, was unprecedentedly sympathetic. 'Horrible man. His wife became a QC just so she'd never have to see him. And quite absurd to imply *William* might be capable of murdering someone, even if he'd ever met the Hamilton boy!'

As I took my leave I met Antonia's gaze for an instant. She wore a strange amused look – as if we were children sharing a secret. I realised she understood everything. Not so much the mere facts, though she was aware I *did* know Dorian, just as she knew I was the connecting element in all the recent deaths and disappearances: Diana, Héctor, Dorian, even Mrs Belsey. More than that, what she dangerously understood was *me*, what I was indeed capable of, and it was clear her measure of this was, like everything else, far more refined than the Camillas of the world.

The question was what I intended to do about it. About her.

22

The 6th Earl of Denzil, Antonia's younger brother, who faced with the scale of his gambling debts quite sensibly drank himself to death, had in short order inherited and then sold the Buckinghamshire family manor. While waiting for Antonia to return with the tea I wondered if any ancestral chattels had slipped through her brother's trembling grasp and ended up in this room, and if so whether I might be able to spot them. Such objects were not likely to be masterpieces of enormous value. Though not unproud to have been described by *The Spectator* as 'England's greatest philistine', the earl possessed a shrewd eye for things that might prolong his legendary lifestyle for another six months, and could be relied on to relinquish them to cash buyers.

What made this little game challenging was finding myself surrounded by items not obscenely expensive or interesting in themselves but which, taken together, exuded unmistakable taste. For every object my eye fell on – serpentine-fronted commode, ormolu Empire mantel clock, van Dyck oil sketch – I'd seen a more elaborate or eccentric or grand version elsewhere. The entire white stucco townhouse, in fact, bore Antonia's strangely distinctive yet absent mark, Harold having abdicated all interest in the property with the exception of his rooms on the fourth floor, which no one (including perhaps his wife) was allowed to visit.

In the same moment she returned with a tea-laden tray – I'd been a guest at the Highclere house many times but it felt strange to be attended to by Antonia herself – I spotted it, the room's surviving inherited chattel. A small khanjar dagger hanging on the wall. Its Y-shaped ivory handle was decorated with gilt floral mounts; between the gold patterning at the hilt and tip, the dark-red velvet covering of the scabbard reminded me in the room's low lighting of Goya's painting of a butchered lamb.

She saw me admire it but said nothing, only smiled faintly.

'Very handsome,' I said. 'I was wondering if it was Persian or perhaps Ottoman.'

'Actually, I think it's Indian. It was a present to my father. I'm afraid I can't remember why or who from.' She set down the tray by bending her knees in a sort of gracefully improvised demi-plié. 'I'm very glad you came over, William. I wanted to thank you for coming to the rescue at Boone's. Poor Roland,' she said, 'perhaps he needs a bit of a rest.'

'It's I who should thank *you*.'

She made no reply to this, but went on pouring the tea with a certain frowning determination. Despite her discomfort it would have been bad manners not to make any reference to the news, discreetly whispered in my ear by István, that Lady Antonia had been pleased to take care of the bill for my table. People liked to gossip about Harold's painstaking scrutiny of his wife's monthly expenditure, which supposedly came out of a modest allowance in relation to their (or rather Harold's) fortune. Even Antonia's most minor transactions, it was said, had to be scrupulously accounted for and explained to her husband.

It was not that, in his meanness, Harold was vindictive or moralistic. In a way he was something worse, or at least more unfortunate: a mix of clinically fastidiousness and helplessly uncomprehending of any sort of material urge. The point was, I couldn't know what degree of inconvenience the several hundred pounds she'd spent on my behalf this evening was going to cause her.

To lighten the mood I enquired about the lapsang souchong. Its smoky flavour, which made me want a cigarette, avoided brashness thanks to a sweet-ish after-note of menthol and roasted pecan.

'I'm so pleased you like it,' Antonia said with genuine enthusiasm. 'Normally I only make it for myself. It's blended with Keemun.'

'Harold is in Somerset, I gather.'

'There was a market cross in Cheddar he wanted to see.' She smiled slightly. 'I think you're the one person I know who not only wouldn't laugh at that, but could muster a clever comment about market crosses. If the circumstances demanded it, I mean. It's funny how you remind me of Harry in some respects.'

Even coming from his wife it required a certain heroic perspective to find the comparison flattering. 'I think Harold has a far more enquiring mind,' I suggested.

'Maybe it's a question of nature as much as degree,' Antonia said delicately. 'My husband's curiosity is very innocent.'

The words were accompanied by a barely visible flush. I'd never before stayed – let alone *arrived* – at her house after 11 p.m., but Antonia hadn't shown any surprise when I appeared at her doorstep. Now she said, with only the faintest show of nerves, how nice it was to have the chance to talk. 'So often we only seem to have a few seconds before being interrupted by someone. Or else we're stuck in a larger group.'

'If I'm completely honest, I'm not sure I've ever had an enjoyable conversation with more than three participants.'

Antonia gave a sad laugh. 'That's a rather frightening perspective on both our lives.'

'I wasn't really complaining. But I suppose it is.'

'Dear William . . .' she said, her tone somehow both vague and deliberative. 'It's funny to think how long we've been friends.'

To most people three years wouldn't merit such a sentimental reflection. (In fact, I'd been trying without success to befriend her for far longer.) Before me they'd come and with equal regularity gone – her 'protégés' as Ingy called them. As Ingy had also made clear, they were usually much younger than I was.

'It's been a great pleasure,' I said.

'Yes, it *has*' – there was a touch of reproach in her earnestness. 'I think it's been one of my greatest. Of course,' she went on carefully, 'I've always understood there are things you'd rather not discuss; about your past, for example. But I've never thought this lessened our friendship. What I'm trying to say is I accept that – I accept *you*.'

For a second time that evening I thanked her.

'I know that just lately you've had to deal with some . . . misfortunes.'

'If you mean my virus,' I said, 'and this silly cut on my forehead—'

'No, not those,' she said, gently but firmly.

'Mrs Belsey, then . . . ?' I found I couldn't stop myself, this delaying of the inevitable.

'I wasn't referring to Judy Belsey,' Antonia replied with the palest flare of impatience. 'Though that was terribly sad.' Her sympathy didn't preclude a sense that the octogenarian's death was not quite *my* tragedy. 'They say you're no longer on good terms with Nikolai. Then there was the awful news about your young friend Dorian Hamilton. And of course the puzzle of your missing goddaughter.'

The words hung in the air.

'I gathered Mrs Belsey had mentioned something about Diana,' I said finally. It felt rather dishonourable to keep referring to my deceased landlady. 'Perhaps Héctor Comala also spoke of her to you.'

Antonia's lips remained parted for a moment, as if caught in two minds. Finally, she said, 'It's rather strange – I haven't heard from him since the party in Belgravia Square. He was meant to come to dinner this evening.'

She remained on the sofa, fragile and angular, while I made a show of wandering casually around the room. It must have been a rather absurd spectacle: with my hands gently locked behind my back I felt like a visiting dignitary. Antonia half followed my movements to show she was neither oblivious to my company nor excessively at home in it.

'Would you mind if I had a look at it? The khanjar dagger.'

It was part of Antonia's genius to make her surprise at my request ('Oh, of course!') seem directed at her own bad manners – in this case, at not having already offered up the object for inspection. It felt light in my fingers, which I splayed delicately to protect the scabbard's velvet covering; already the wood was visible in odd patches.

'May I . . . ?' Without waiting for a reply I eased out the blade, which curved once and then re-curved at the tip in a fluid shape, like the squiggle of a Spanish 'ñ'. Too late I vaguely remembered that drawing these ceremonial daggers was considered taboo, in the Middle East at any rate. The point, not sharp but not blunt either, left a white furrow down the pad of my index finger, bifurcating the web (a legacy of years of idle bathing) of finely etched lines.

'I think I *will* have a second cup of tea, even though it means I won't sleep. Sorry,' Antonia said, 'I seem to be babbling.'

'Don't apologise. I'm always happy to listen to you.'

She gave a shudder, barely perceptible, at my vulgar remark. Or perhaps it was too much what she wanted to hear.

'I wouldn't blame you for not believing me,' I said, 'but for once I'm telling the truth.'

'William, you're bleeding! Your finger.'

I brushed my pricked finger with my thumb, frowning at the resulting smear. 'That was stupid of me.'

'Do you need a tissue?'

'No, no – thank you,' I said distractedly. I put the dagger down on the commode to retrieve my handkerchief from inside my jacket. (Parading such a banal item in one's top pocket had always struck me as an odd custom.) I was reflecting I had no means to pay for the dry cleaning of the bloodied Charvet silk when Antonia said she didn't know I was left-handed.

'Oh, I'm not—'

Immediately I realised my error. For a moment we both stared at the ivory handle of the dagger, which despite its relative weightlessness I hadn't risked gripping with my right hand. Even simple activities, like drinking tea, needed to be carefully managed to ensure my left hand could play a covertly dominant role.

'Are you sure you don't want to take your jacket off?' Antonia's voice was steady enough, though there was a trace of agitation in the way her finger felt along the silver chain of a Joan of Arc pendant, the only adornment to her black silk dress. 'It's quite warm this evening.'

I was quite comfortable, thank you, I told her. 'You must be wondering why I'm visiting you so late.'

'It was a lovely surprise, as I mentioned.'

I went on, 'You must be wondering too about the various misfortunes you brought up. Whether they might all in some strange way be connected.'

'Again as I said earlier' – glancing at the resting dagger – 'I would never want to pry into your affairs.'

'You did say that. But perhaps it wouldn't be fair – perhaps it can no longer hold, our friendship I mean, if I keep leaving you in the dark.'

'There are so *many* things we've never discussed. We wouldn't have time to cover it all in one evening.'

'Nevertheless – perhaps there's something in particular on your mind.'

I continued waiting, even after it seemed clear she wasn't going to speak.

'Well,' she said, eventually, 'ever since you arrived in London things have been said about you.'

'I see. May I ask what?'

'That you're a liar and a thief. That you betrayed your country and can't go back there. That you're charming and lazy and thoroughly malign.'

'I see,' I said again.

'Of course I didn't pay attention to any of it,' she said. 'When we became friends I never stopped inviting you to things, introducing you to people. You could say I've risked everything on you – my whole reputation. Harold's too.'

'I'm grateful,' I said, feeling as I spoke the words that I really meant them. 'For what it's worth you've made it all bearable for me, the last few years.'

There was a stretch of silence, long enough almost to start to relax into it.

'We keep complimenting each other, in our peculiar way,' Antonia said with a twitch of a smile. She let go of the silver chain. 'I'm worried I'll spoil everything if I try it again.'

My finger had stopped bleeding. Carefully, I folded the handkerchief and put it away, making sure that the unstained sections of silk were those pressing against the suit pocket lining. 'As usual I think you're right,' I said. 'There really seems nothing left to say. Damn,' I said, picking up the dagger. 'I've left a spot of blood on the handle.'

I put the thin edge of my tongue to my thumb and cleaned the red smudge from the dagger's ivory grip.

'Well, perhaps not everything,' Antonia said a fraction quickly.

I saw she was afraid but there was perhaps too an element of excitement, of the sort she had no doubt felt in her encounters with Héctor.

'No?' I said.

'It's something that's been coming for a while. I haven't known quite how to mention it. We do so rarely have the chance to speak in private.'

I waited.

'Well, it's Harry – or rather Harry and me. I'm leaving him.'

Part V

23

I was spending the afternoon in the company of a banker, a fortyish Dutchman with broad provincial features from a van Ostade painting. We were in an upper-level bar-restaurant of a skyscraper. He insisted on ordering us both a steady flow of Old Fashioneds infused with Kobe beef fat while he spoke about the art he wanted me to acquire for his new house in Cap Ferrat – 'For sure some Chinese stuff,' he said, with a gulp of cocktail. He'd read a *Forbes* article on the burgeoning Sino market. I told him I regrettably didn't read *Forbes*, but he waved a great fleshy hand: 'My girl will send you the piece.' Also, he went on, maybe a Koons or two. Nothing wild in form or price. He seemed not to hear when I said I didn't think Koons was quite in his budget. Instead he told me his wife had just arrived in Paris: it was short notice but could I arrange for her to be on the guest list for one or two of the couture week parties? The kind – he was emphatic on this point – attended by 'celebrities'.

I was only half-listening to him. The place had been full when we arrived, though by 3 p.m. the bar area was thinning out. With one exception, the afternoon boozers were a usual enough mix: a scattering of tourist couples, dominated by a large group of City bores.

At a table by the wall-to-floor window a solitary man sipped a Brahma beer. It was his second; the first had taken him an hour to finish. Loose flesh spilled over his shirt collar in a manner with which, like his cheap grey suit, I was now disconcertingly familiar.

Occasionally he glanced around at the Latin–Asian décor with a faintly incredulous air. Or he would turn to inspect the Swiss Re building, gleaming below us like a Fabergé bowling pin. Not once – despite our proximity and the relative lack of human activity in the room – did he look in my direction. He had no book or smartphone to occupy his attention.

It occurred to me that I'd seen this jowly gentleman many times in the last few weeks, but at no point had another human being verified his existence to me. Was he flesh and blood? Or some awful mental apparition?

The banker was talking about his recent decision to join the board of a Netherlands football club. It was very successful, he assured me, and the team regularly finished in a top position in the Eredivisie. But it was not the one he had supported since boyhood! He leaned back in his chair and erupted with laughter, eclipsing the noise from the braying group, one or two of whom shot jealous glances in our direction.

I decided it was too risky to steer the conversation towards my ghoulish shadow. If he turned out to be a figment of my imagination, it wouldn't be a strong incentive for the banker to retain my services and I sorely needed the cash advance we had spoken of. On the other hand, if he *was* real, it hardly seemed sensible to encourage the banker gauchely to stare at him.

After a small eternity the Dutchman looked around and checked his watch and announced (it didn't seem particularly wise, given the quantity of bourbon he'd just consumed) that he would go directly to the gym. The man by the window responded by signalling for the bill. After paying he didn't leave but continued sitting in the same unoccupied fashion.

Inside the glass-box lift, the banker stuck a hand out to prevent the doors closing on my dogged follower. His slow-witted agrarian visage showed no recognition of the new entrant when he announced with relish, 'This thing drops like a stone!'

At close quarters I realised the man joining us was a few years older than me. Notwithstanding his appalling suit, his tubbiness, his thinning hair and oily wrinkled skin, there was an obvious intelligence about him which transcended his shambolic appearance and gave him an aura of confidence and even, albeit perversely, of stylishness.

'I was just thinking of Orpheus,' the jowly one said. His accent was as I'd imagined: English, cheerful, minor public school.

'Aha . . . ! *Ja, ja* . . . !' said the banker with uncharacteristic hesitancy.

'On his way to Hades.'

The Englishman looked directly at me for the first time. His intentions were ostensibly innocent: to include me politely in the conversation, and perhaps assure himself his classical allusion wasn't a misjudgement. I couldn't help noticing the cold appraising eyes above the amicable grin.

'Gluck,' I said, returning his smile and thinking this evening I might open a bottle of red and revisit *Orphée et Eurydice*.

He pointed to a liberal emergence of hairs at the entrance of his ear. 'I'm afraid I'm terribly deaf.'

'Good luck. For this plunging lift, I mean.'

When we emerged on Bishopsgate there seemed a danger that the banker, in a fit of indiscriminate sociability, was going to insist the three of us share a taxi together. To pre-empt this possibility I gestured back at Houndsditch and announced I was headed in that direction. Fortunately, the banker hadn't asked about my afternoon plans, so if I now sounded impolitely vague there was no chance I was going to be caught in a lie. His parting nod in the direction of the Englishman and me left the sense that he couldn't quite remember which of us he'd just commissioned to spend a million pounds on dubious art. With my Hamilton leather briefcase, I might have been another broker or lawyer on my way to a meeting. I turned into one of those Dickensian side streets, which despite the invasion of glass and steel still veined the City. In my early years in London I had more than once got lost down such alleys: finding myself, rather to my surprise, standing before a hidden sunlit courtyard, or dingy sixteenth-century pub with great Hodgkin daubs of colour emerging from hanging baskets and tubs, or else a dead-end of rubbish bins and ventilation units.

Now, however, I had a very precise idea where I was. The narrow street was cool in the shade, and virtually silent

218

– that late afternoon lull before the workers escaped their desks to enjoy a beer in the last of the sunshine. The only sound was of a familiar figure trailing at an insolently short distance behind me.

After about a hundred yards I spotted the discreet iron staircase. My feet as I descended clanged in a manner I found oppressively loud, even though it was very much my intention to signal where I was going.

24

Jaume, the barman at Le Tartin, put some Krug on ice. We spoke in Catalan, an old joke neither of us quite had the heart to abandon.

'Shall I bring the bottle to your usual spot?'

'Yes – in the, ah, corner.' My primitive grasp of the language was of course the source of the amusement. 'And for now a vodka.'

He poured from a bottle of Royal Dragon. 'If your tastes weren't so expensive, your drinks would be on the house.'

'You may say this of me when I'm dead' – I didn't know the word for 'epitaph', so it came out a more straightfor-wardly morbid reflection than I'd intended. On my way to the corner booth I turned and said, 'Two glasses for the champagne. A friend is just arriving.'

He sat down as if we were indeed old friends who didn't bother with proper greetings. He looked around without making a show of it, the way people often do; but quickly, absorbing everything.

'It's nice to see a barman in black tie. I don't know the City well, but this feels more like how they used to do things, before the Big Bang and so on. I suppose that's another way of saying before the Americans came along. No offence. Ah . . . !' the Englishman exclaimed non-committally, at the sight of Jaume arriving with the Krug in an ice bucket. 'I see you're moving on from the Russian stuff.'

'It was only a palette cleanser – the "Russian stuff", as you call it.'

Jaume poured champagne for my guest and me. When he finished I thanked him and confirmed we didn't need anything else for the moment.

Without glancing at his flute, the Englishman leaned forward and, frowning with great interest, asked if that was Catalan he'd just heard.

I nodded. 'Well, in fact Jaume is from Valencia, so technically it was Valencian.'

'Ah, *is* he! And are those – I mean, Catalan and Valencian – separate to the Balearic dialects?'

'As I understand it the differences between all of them are very subtle, as much political as linguistic. I was in Minorca recently—'

He nodded in a friendly manner. 'Yes, I know.'

'I noticed they'd changed all the road signs from Castilian. My driver told me they were now in standard Catalan rather than Minorcan. The locals were even more fed up than they'd been before.'

'So often that's the way,' he said cheerily. 'The old *Narzissmus der kleinen Differenzen.*'

His German accent was close to flawless. He saw me absorb it, this unexpected flash of – where exactly? Bonn. Even East Berlin perhaps. He smiled at his little slip. 'It feels rather odd that this is our first conversation,' he said.

'How's that?'

'I feel I already know you – quite well, to be frank. Probably it doesn't surprise you to learn I've been following your career for some time. But of course it's not the same for you. One tends to forget.'

'There is a certain visual familiarity,' I said with what I hoped was only a touch of rancour.

'Yes, of course! I suppose you've seen me around a bit lately. Sorry about that.'

'It seemed rather old fashioned.'

'Oh, certainly. But then *you're* rather old fashioned. No mobile phone. Never use a computer.' He leaned forward in the booth again with hunched shoulders – he had terrible posture. 'Also my doctor has been nagging me to take more exercise.'

I took a sip of champagne. 'I admit it never occurred to me you were following me around to improve your health and well-being. As opposed to degrading mine.'

'Well, of course,' he agreed, 'there's that too. But really I wanted to make myself available for when you were ready to talk – and here we are.'

'What should I call you, by the way?'

'Call me Erskine.'

'Any reason?'

He grinned. 'I did think of changing it at one point. Some colleagues seem to view my name as an affront to the modern ethos. But it would have been hard on one's old friends, don't you think?'

'It's hard for me to say. I don't really have anyone in that category.'

'No . . .' he said reflectively. 'Of course William *was* your old friend, wasn't he?'

I frowned and said I didn't follow.

'Your name is Dwight Hoffer – do correct me if I'm wrong. William Hastings was your room-mate at West Point.'

Another silence, less amicable.

'A Boston Brahmin, I gather; very charming and urbane. But I'm bringing up painful memories.'

'More than anything,' I said, 'I'm impressed at your thoroughness.'

With an impertinence that surprised me he reached over and tapped a podgy finger against the face of my watch.

'I have a feeling those old Omegas were occasionally assigned by the US military.'

They were, but I said nothing.

'Wasn't his father a distinguished pilot?'

'Who are we talking about?'

'Hastings. Or rather his father.'

I watched the neat columns of bubbles in my flute. In my mind the claret walls of this place, its starched tablecloths and frilly lamps, had a comforting association with Singer Sargent's *Dinner Table at Night*. 'It was a long time ago. I really don't remember.'

'No, of course,' he said in his soft chipper voice. 'I believe it's the case, though, that the death of William Hastings marked the end of your West Point career. Not long after that you surfaced in Mexico.'

'And what about you?' I said.

'Me?'

'I'd guess you were from Sussex.'

He hunched forward again. 'West or East?'

'I'll say West.'

224

'Oh, bad luck! My parents' home was near Wadhurst. Which school?'

Another sip of champagne. 'It's between Lancing and King's, Canterbury. Perhaps Tonbridge.'

'That's very good.'

'Which was it?'

'King's.'

'And then Oxford.'

'Yes,' he said, 'then Oxford.'

'Probably a smaller college – somewhere traditional, not too intimidating for a sensitive young man, with eminent history dons. I assume that's what you studied.'

He nodded. I said the name of a college.

'As I say,' Erskine said, his smile fading a little, 'very good.'

'I suppose you were taught by Denby-Powell. Probably he recommended you.'

'Despite my reasonable German he was quite keen I become a medievalist.'

After a short lull, I said, 'You don't know Harold Highclere, by any chance?'

'Highclere! Oh no – we hardly inhabit the same milieu.'

This remark or rather its prickly undertone surprised me, not least since Afrikaner Harold probably wanted nothing so much as to be Erskine. I didn't point this out, but simply said I didn't think Harold was in anyone's milieu as such.

'You'd know more about that than me. Though I do hear he's something of a scholar.'

'In any case, I meant Denby-Powell must have recommended you for MI5.'

'Ah. Now you've said it. Part of me can't help thinking that's a shame.'

'Why's that?'

'It puts our burgeoning friendship at risk.'

'I'm not sure either of us is really the sentimental sort.'

'No, perhaps you're right,' Erskine said, taking his first sip of Krug. 'Shall we make a start then?'

25

'We know about Héctor Comala. It's only fair to make that clear.'

'I doubt it's quite true.'

'That we intend to be fair?'

'That you know about him.'

When Erskine spoke again his voice had become chilly and business-like. 'Before London he was with the Mexican Federal Ministerial Police, formerly the Federal Investigation Agency. He had connections with the Ortega organisation; the rumour was Nicolas José himself rescued him from a probably brief life of petty thievery. By all accounts he had expensive tastes, was clever and cultivated but essentially vicious. His life became more complicated after the senior Ortega's death.' He paused. 'What have I missed?'

'That's most of it,' I conceded. 'Apart from the obvious.' Even in an empty bar, he wasn't going to risk displeasing the Agency by referring to my old professional connection with Héctor.

'Ah, perhaps you mean what really complicated Comala's existence.'

'What was that?'

'*You*. I can see you're thinking it was the other way round, that if it weren't for Comala disturbing your new life in London we wouldn't be having this discussion. So I suppose there are two ways of looking at the fact that you're here and he isn't.'

'Nor is Dorian Hamilton,' I pointed out.

Cocking his head slightly, Erskine leant back in the booth to stare at a spot near my feet. 'I couldn't help noticing that's a Hamilton suitcase.'

I'd owned it for years, I explained.

'That's exactly what I told my colleagues – a coincidence! I must say it's a distinguished-looking object. Rather outside my budget, of course' – again the surprising bourgeois chagrin – 'though that spring-lock reminds me of my old prep school trunk.'

'Your colleagues didn't believe you?'

'It was more they considered it poor taste. A provocation, almost.'

'I think you know I didn't kill Dorian Hamilton.'

'As it happens I believe that's probably true,' Erskine said. 'Just as Comala's death was most likely self-defence.'

I gave a little nod. I was oddly moved by this show of faith.

'Which is not to say,' he went on, 'that there aren't always arguments. Or that left to their own devices the investigating authorities wouldn't arrive at a different set of conclusions. In the case of Dorian Hamilton, for example, there seems to be a margin of doubt as to whether the young man was falling when he encountered Comala's knife.'

'You're suggesting I tripped the boy?'

228

'Or pushed him in the back. Either way,' he went on breezily, 'one could speculate it was an instinctive thing. Perhaps you warned poor Hamilton to leave and he didn't listen. In that moment you realised – or your brain, your reflexes did – that a few extra seconds might save your life. What that means for the *mens rea* question I'll leave to the lawyers.'

Jaume wandered over to see about topping us up. I gestured with my palm and he retreated back to the bar.

'As you can imagine,' Erskine went on, 'that's by no means the extent of your evidential difficulties.'

'Incidentally,' I said, from an instinctive urge to discomfort him in return, 'I haven't seen any mention of Comala in the papers.'

'. . . I'm referring to camera footage from the Ritz and so on. Then there's the young lady. Diana Domínguez Saavedra. Her phone's GPS records show she visited Onslow Square shortly before she went missing.'

I plucked the dripping Krug from the ice bucket and held it unwisely aloft.

Erskine declined with a flicker of distaste. 'On the day she disappeared she left her phone behind – almost as if she were following specific instructions. For what it's worth I think you tried to make her understand she was in danger from Héctor Comala. You knew her father, I imagine, in Mexico?'

'He's an associate of Igor Ortega, loosely speaking.'

He gave a quick nod. 'I'm afraid it's a past tense situation.'

'Ah – I didn't know for sure. Rafael wasn't the worst sort of man,' I said – not one of the great eulogies.

'In that case I'll spare you the details.'

'I can imagine them well enough. But thank you.'

Even in the dim light Erskine's forehead was distractingly oily. He shifted his weight, like an impatient schoolboy. 'The important thing, as I'm sure you've understood, is that we'd like to help you.'

'You're offering to protect me from Igor Ortega?' I couldn't restrain the note of sarcasm.

'Among others, yes. We can certainly do that.'

I drank the rest of the champagne in my glass. 'I'm sorry. I would have liked to help, not least because I'm fond of this country and I appreciate this must be a rather embarrassing situation for you.'

'"Embarrassing" in what sense?' His tolerant grin seemed to suggest if anyone were making a fool of himself it was me.

'A bilateral initiative ruined by a murderous attaché working for a drug cartel: it might be enough to bring the government down.'

'I don't know about that!' Erskine laughed. 'They survive far worse things in DF.'

'I meant here in London, if there was any suggestion you colluded in a cover-up.'

His mirth gave way to a hard impatient stare. In a voice that stopped short of an outright whisper, which might have attracted the attention of Jaume, he said, 'This isn't about saving the Mexicans' blushes, though they were very happy to play along with the "cover-up", as you call it – a business, incidentally, which became rather easier after the death of your landlady. I suppose she might have seen Diana visiting your flat? In any case,' he continued, 'our actions

– or perhaps I should say the collective restraint of the British state, at least for the time being – have nothing to do with Comala or bilateral initiatives. They've been about protecting you.'

It wasn't a surprise the security services might 'oversee' a police investigation for reasons of overriding national interest. There was one thing I didn't understand, however. 'I'm not much use to you. I'm no longer friendly with the Russian, as you must know.'

'Then you might consider finding another one!' He pushed at the base of his champagne glass, spilling some of its contents onto the tablecloth. As if regretting the little show of intemperance, he dabbed at the wet patch with a napkin. 'I wonder if all this makes you feel rather nostalgic,' he said in a sly, ruminative tone. 'After all, the Cold War was where your career started, and now suddenly you're rather in demand again.'

'Perhaps that's true for both of us.'

He set out the terms of the offer. In exchange for protection from various parties, including the Metropolitan Police, they wanted a regular stream of intelligence about the mood inside the Kremlin. Logical enough: the remaining oligarchs were as ruthlessly committed to knowing the tsaral mind as they were to anything else they deemed essential to their survival. More than that, the British security services wanted whatever I could give them on an array of subjects: the FSB; Russian organised crime in the United Kingdom; the byzantine nexus (focusing chiefly on drugs and arms trafficking) between Russia's spies and her mafia and Al-Qaeda. If the relationship proved satisfactory, on top of supposedly saving my skin they were prepared to pay me a regular consulting fee. The amount was to be discussed at a later date, and would naturally depend on the value of whatever information I provided, but in the order of a couple of thousand pounds a month.

I'd meant it when I told Erskine I had a certain affection for England, but in the end it wasn't a difficult decision. We both knew he and his colleagues couldn't really guarantee my safety. For another thing, the money was not close to sufficient. Antonia and I were getting by on my occasional commissions for small fry like the Dutch banker, combined with her allowance from Harold. The modesty of that stipend wasn't vindictiveness on Harold's part. In fact he had reacted to events as well as any man might be expected to in his shoes. He simply couldn't grasp why she might need more funds, which was anyway, of course, a long-standing source of marital unease.

Our impoverished circumstances – as yet Antonia and I had no plan for where we were going to live after the sale of the Onslow Square flat next month, Annabel Belsey having acted on her intention with expected gimlet-eyed efficiency – were to me unspeakably shameful. In such a context, twenty-odd thousand pounds a year from MI5 were not going to solve anything.

Besides, or perhaps most importantly, my reputation was all I had. That applied for Erskine and his associates as much as prospective clients. If they chose to leave me alone 'for the time being', to echo the Englishman's jaunty threat, it was because they believed they could depend on my discretion. (I'd made a mistake with my foolish reference to bringing down the British government, which fortunately Erskine appeared to have dismissed for the bluff it was.)

No, my best bet was to string them along, at least in the short term: to decline their offer, but not so categorically that they would give up on me, and not without carefully heeding Erskine's advice about making interesting new friends, all the while hoping for some miracle solution to present itself. My instinct told me that if such a miracle were to arrive from anywhere it would be from Antonia.

I waited long enough for my answer to seep in.

'You think you don't need to worry about me,' Erskine said.

'Not at all. You were already on my list of problems.'

'Perhaps not unrelatedly' – his tone had suddenly lightened, a gentleman in (temporary) defeat – 'I gather you're involved these days. In the romantic vein.'

'I may as well confirm it, since I've no one else to tell.'

He looked a little embarrassed.

'I did say I hadn't any old friends.'

'Well, as long as I don't have to give the best man's speech – if it comes to that.'

'The awful thing is I suppose I'd have to ask Gianni Bardoni.'

'Yes – I suppose you would, now that Roland Turner is not so much in the frame,' he said. I couldn't get used to a stranger being so casually familiar with the details of my life. 'I gather he's been rather shaken up by recent events,' Erskine added.

'Mostly by the fact no one calls him much any more. He's very sociable by nature.'

'That was certainly my impression. From what I gathered,' the spy said with distaste, 'he made his fortune by being insatiably convivial.'

26

We arrived at the Grosvenor House just before seven. There was time, I hoped, for a quick drink at the bar before visiting the emir.

Inside the hotel young women in elbow-length gloves and tiaras and white gowns decorated with Venice lace were converging on the ballroom. Their powdered relatives watched on without regard for the obstruction they were causing the regular guests.

I was impatient to cut through the crowd – I didn't want to have to skip the aperitif. My companion had already sensed my mood. Though two decades older and hidden inside a long black coat, its collar upturned at the neck, Antonia easily surpassed the debutantes. I'd long ago decided the secret of her allure was that her face had a way of conveying two opposing qualities – just now, shy self-possession – in subtle and shifting relation. It was why it was so hard to picture her in her absence, and why she never looked the same in two photos or paintings. Nor was it only artists who were drawn to her. The idea of Antonia as a fugitive presence wasn't separate to the urge to lock her in a cage, not least when she seemed, in her characteristically paradoxical fashion, so keen to clamber in, providing – it was not a trivial caveat – the gilding was sufficiently magnificent.

I trailed in her wake as the crowd of normally un-obliging Russians parted before her. At one point I reached out and placed my hand lightly on her forearm: she immediately paused in her tracks. 'I wouldn't mind stopping at the bar,' I said. 'What do you think?' I was certain that she didn't want to risk being late for the emir.

'Absolutely, if that's what you want.' With a look of great seriousness, but smiling a fraction, she added, 'Perhaps just quickly.'

Moments later I almost bumped into Nikolai's young assistant, Maksim. He was loitering with a tall gentleman with a flowing Tolstoyan beard and scarlet sash.

'Hello, Maksim.'

'William Hoffer! I heard somewhere you'd left town.' He glanced hungrily at Antonia. 'We must have a drink later.'

I gestured to my absent dinner jacket. 'We're just passing through.'

'Are you sure? I imagine you're rather a natural at the waltz.'

'Sorry. Good luck though.'

'What for?'

'Well, you're debbing, aren't you?'

The Tolstoyan companion laughed throatily.

'Not me!' Maksim, who had turned slightly pink, put his fingertips to his thinning hair. 'I'm twenty-eight, you know.'

He wouldn't forgive me for teasing him, but he was a silly boy who already disliked me. Besides I knew I would not be allowed near Nikolai again. On a whim, I turned back to Maksim. 'How's Yulia Azarova, by the way?'

He looked at me curiously for a moment. Then his interest passed (it was why he'd never be useful to Nikolai) and he gave a little shrug. 'Didn't work out,' he said, turning conclusively back to the older gent.

When he visited London the emir usually took the top two floors at the Dorchester. The Grosvenor House was the next hotel along on Park Lane, and similarly convenient for Al Hamra and other popular spots with moneyed Arabs – though in fact he was said to bring his own chef with him, and rarely left his opulent enclave. I'd never met him myself. The failure felt less lacerating ever since the emir came up in conversation with an Egyptian acquaintance of mine who, fleeing the Revolution, had slept at the Dorchester every night for two years. In all that time, he told me, he had never so much as laid eyes on the reclusive multi-billionaire.

The Russian ball explained why the emir switched hotels for this London visit. A number of Princess Romanoff's guests of honour would no doubt be slipping off after dinner, as the band struck up Tchaikovsky's polonaise and the dancing got underway, to visit the highest floor. As he so rarely received visitors the emir would have a crowded schedule; even Antonia, with all her charm and connections, had only managed to secure me ten minutes.

The large and peopled penthouse lounge felt like what it was: a luxury hotel within a luxury hotel. In the brief time before someone arrived to usher her to the emira's suite I worried, quite needlessly, that Antonia might betray some sign of discomfort at being the only female presence in the room.

Two dozen or so vassals or courtiers or general hangers-on – men at any rate of my profession – brazenly watched as I picked up an *Economist* from an illumined bank of magazines and took one of the free armchairs. The man opposite me wore a silk suit with large gold buttons engraved with Versace medusa heads. He didn't answer my *Good evening.*

We had arrived a couple of minutes late, to Antonia's silent consternation. I wondered first if this marginal tardiness had earned me a black mark, and then as time dragged on if my presence hadn't been registered by the right people. Had I missed my slot?

It was merely nerves, however. Deep down I knew the involvement of the emir's wife, even only indirectly via Antonia, guaranteed I would be granted an audience.

He seemed under the misapprehension that Antonia and I were engaged to be married. Or perhaps it was a matter of cultural delicacy. Regardless, his congratulations, offered without shifting his attention from a Gulf television news channel, were appropriately flat. She was not after all even legally divorced – had not, though the emir did not know this, explicitly spoken of such an intention – and I (at fifty-one!) an old bachelor. 'Will you become a Lord? Lord – Hoffer?'

I decided to go along with his question, despite feeling uneasy about my relative lack of experience of Arabs of his rank. Did he already know the answer? Was he indifferent to how vulgar he sounded? 'The title is hers alone,' I said.

'She will be Lady Antonia Hoffer?'

'Exactly.'

He thought about this. 'And you are still Mister Hoffer.'

'That's right,' I said, a slight tightness creeping into my voice.

The emir was sprawled out on a large sofa, an oversize remote control nestled in his fat palm. Sitting at a nearby chair, legs crossed, was a rake-thin man with delicate Levantine features. He wore rather prissy rimless spectacles which he removed and began to wipe with the tip of his narrow tie.

There seemed an expectation I should say something. I began a rambling sort of pitch, where I tried to convey my usefulness in managing certain burdens associated with the possession of an unimaginable fortune, though it was no doubt clear to both men that I was not personally familiar with this predicament. In the matter of art, I gave what I hoped was a sense of catholic expertise, covering acquisition for investment, questions of philanthropy and public relations, and so on. I didn't bother to mention the money-laundering aspect, mostly because the emir was far too rich to involve himself in that sort of business.

After I finished there was a silence.

'I have people for these things,' the emir said. His gaze did not stray from the widescreen television above the fireplace.

'Then I'm sorry. I think there's been a misunderstanding.'

The emir glanced in the direction of the bespectacled adviser. I assumed I was to be ushered from the suite, but abruptly he resumed speaking. 'A Russian – a Jew, I think – wanted to buy an oil company in his country. He approached Western banks to raise money, but they told him he was mad. The company had many debts. But the main problem was the town where this company was located was lawless, which is to say it was administered by local criminals.' The emir's eyes – glistening but lifeless, like wet coffee beans – were on me at last. 'You're familiar with this story?'

'I think so,' I said.

'Do you know what the company was worth, five years after the Russian bought it?'

'Enough to give those bankers sleepless nights. Though it's also true the company doesn't exist any more, and things didn't ultimately pan out well for the acquirer – or the mayor of the town, if I remember.' I wondered how often the emir heard even mildly dissenting views.

For the first time the adviser spoke. 'His Excellency is offering you a stake in a new joint venture. Shale.'

'I see,' I said. 'May I ask who the other partners are?'

He touched the tip of his finger lightly to each rim of his spectacles. The slow, almost priestly gesture conveyed a certain offence had been taken. 'They prefer to remain confidential at this time. I'm sure you understand.'

'What size equity are you proposing?'

'For you, very small. Less than one per cent.'

Neither man was fooled by my attempt to react casually, as if I received these sorts of offers all the time. They knew that given the scale of the emir's energy investments it was the payday I'd been waiting for my whole life.

'We're also prepared to advance an immediate loan,' the adviser continued, 'against part of the value of your shares.'

'Their value now,' I asked, with a great effort at indifference, 'or for when I would be authorised to sell them under the share agreement?'

The emir turned up the volume of the television slightly.

'The lawyers can discuss all these details with you,' the adviser replied. 'Subject to that, we're ready to sign the documents tonight. The funds would reach your wife's account tomorrow.'

'My . . . fiancée, you mean?' I had an uneasy feeling my spur-of-the-moment lie was going to have troublesome consequences.

The adviser put on a rather affected show of boredom, scratching his cheek and sighing at his shoes. We were both aware I'd fallen into a trap. 'It's best to make these transfers to a trusted third party, as you know. Obviously you should get married as soon as possible. For now, it's enough to give your agreement in principle – as a gentleman.'

'I understand. And I'm grateful for the offer. I do, however, have a couple of supplementary questions which I consider of great importance.'

I was half afraid the two men could hear the blood pounding in my neck. Addressing the emir directly, I asked, 'Will the shale exploration primarily be in Mexico?'

Again it was the adviser who answered. 'Primarily.'

'The state of Tamaulipas?'

'We'll be focusing on the Tampico-Misantla basin. That includes Tamaulipas, of course.'

'And you'd like to send me there – to Matamoros – to see if an agreement can be reached with the local . . . non-state authorities.'

'Was that a third question?' said the adviser with a razorous smile. 'His Excellency has another meeting now. I have already mentioned the lawyers are waiting to take you through the draft agreements, in as much detail as you wish.'

It was unlikely I would return from such a trip: that was a gamble they – emir and adviser – were comfortable with. The emir needed to diversify into new areas of the global energy market. If shale was the future, why not own that too? Perhaps Mexico *would* turn out to be too lawless. They were not cowboys and this was not the Old West. On the other hand, my head on a plate might mollify Igor Ortega enough to listen to the emir's next messenger. They may or may not have considered how the various American agencies would respond to my return to Mexico, though either way it would be a problem for me.

A more immediate question was whether they were aware not only of my past as a cartel intermediary, but that I'd recently killed a member of the Ortega payroll in London. It was possible they'd even decided this last fact might, from Igor's unhinged perspective, be taken as sufficient proof of character to grant me an audience with the *patrón* himself, just as years ago Héctor had earned a hearing with Nicolas José Ortega by murdering the latter's bodyguard.

Something else: what, or who, had encouraged them to believe I might be desperate enough to contemplate such a perilous offer?

The sound of the suite door opening behind me confirmed my time was up. As I rose to my feet, I caught a glimpse of Antonia waiting just beyond the threshold of the room. She was with a tall glamorous woman in a cream Armani suit and discreet hijab. Antonia's expression wasn't quite readable – unusually anxious, perhaps, or impatient. Excited.

Well played, I wanted to say to her. If things went badly for me she would no doubt return to Harold, of whom she was really quite fond, with a pleasing boost to her personal funds. (I somehow doubted the emir would recall a 'loan' deposited in Antonia's account.) And in the unlikely event that my Mexican venture succeeded, she and I would resume our new partnership in a more economically promising situation.

'I can't sit down with any lawyers this evening,' I said to the adviser. 'I have dinner plans.'

'Tomorrow then – first thing?'

I thought for a few seconds. An old Spanish *dicho* came to mind, something Héctor used to say: *Con dinero baila el perro*. Money makes the dog dance.

'Just one lawyer will be enough. Tell him to come to Onslow Square. Or wait . . .' I was aware of the emir's attention from the sofa, but my own focus was on the doorway and, just beyond that, the rigid outline of Antonia. Her habitual graceful smile seemed now to have a faintly imploring quality. Then suddenly – the movement was so quick and discreet I wondered for an instant if I had imagined it – she gave a little nod of the head, from which I understood that while she'd cleverly hedged her bets she was not indifferent to my decision. She wanted me to accept her challenge – and perhaps even survive. I turned back to the emir's adviser. 'Make it sometime after lunch.' There seemed no point spoiling my leisurely morning routine, the bath and Mozart and G and T. Later, I'd be packing a Hamilton suitcase. Except perhaps I wouldn't go to Mexico directly. A short detour via my country of birth might be interesting, if not without its own risks. For the authorities my presence was even less welcome in the United States than it was on the other side of the border, and it was also true that certain criminal investigations from West Point, albeit from half a lifetime ago, remained theoretically unclosed. But given who ultimately awaited me in Matamoros, what had I really to lose?

The prodigal son! My spirits lifted at the thought I might persuade Antonia to accompany me on the trip. Together, I felt giddily certain we would be rather a triumph: that Manhattan society, the CIA, Igor Ortega himself – the New World and everything in it – could not fail to bend to our collective charm.

ACKNOWLEDGEMENTS

I'm extremely grateful to Karolina Sutton and Mark Richards. I'd also like to thank Arts Council England for their support of this book.